Just William's Luck

also published by
Macmillan Children's B

An invitation from William

Join my club and becum a n Outlaw

William Brown

You can join the Outlaws Club!
You will receive
✳ a special Outlaws wallet containing
your own Outlaws badge
the Club Rules
and
a letter from William giving you the secret password

To join the Club send a letter with your name and address written in block capitals telling us you want to join the Outlaws, and a postal order for 45p, to

The Outlaws Club
577 Kingston Road
Raynes Park
LONDON SW20 8SA

You must live in the United Kingdom or the Republic of Ireland in order to join.

Just William's Luck

RICHMAL CROMPTON

Illustrated by Thomas Henry

MACMILLAN CHILDREN'S BOOKS

First published 1948

Copyright Richmal C. Ashbee

The illustrations by Thomas Henry are reproduced by permission
of the Hamlyn Group Picture Library.

First published in this edition 1989 by

MACMILLAN CHILDREN'S BOOKS
A division of Macmillan Publishers Limited
London and Basingstoke
Associated companies throughout the world

ISBN 0-333-51097-6

A CIP catalogue record for this book is available from the British
Library.

Typeset by Matrix, 21 Russell Street, London WC2

Printed and bound in Great Britain by
Cox & Wyman Ltd, Reading

Chapter 1

Mr. Heppleback, the glazier, cycled slowly down the country lane and in at the gate of the small detached house in which the Brown family lived. His practised eye swept the scene before him, coming to rest finally on a shattered pane of glass in a window on the right of the door. He nodded to himself with an expression of mingled amusement and resignation, then dismounted, unstrapped the sheet of glass from the back of his cycle and rang the bell.

A middle-aged woman, wearing an overall, opened the door. She had a flat expressionless face, and she looked at Mr. Heppleback without apparent interest.

" 'Mornin', Emily," said Mr. Heppleback. "How's yourself?"

"Might be worse," said Emily in a voice that doubted it.

Mr. Heppleback cocked his head over his shoulder.

"Dining-room window again, I see?"

" 'Again' 's the word," said Emily with a sigh.

Mr. Heppleback took his foot rule from his pocket and began to measure the window-pane.

"Well, boys will be boys," he said. "That's what I always say."

"It's not what Mr. Brown says," said Emily, lingering in the doorway to watch Mr. Heppleback's activities with a lack-lustre eye. " 'E says somethin' quite different to that. Took quite a while, too, sayin' it las' night."

"What was it this time? A cricket ball?"

"No, Big Chief Firewater's tomahawk."

Mr. Heppleback laughed. "You don't say!" he said. He put his foot rule back into his pocket and surveyed the garden.

"Not a bad bit o' garden this, you know," he said. "Pity they don't keep it tidier."

"How d'you mean, 'tidier'?" said Emily.

"Well . . . look at that flower-bed."

"Oh that!" said Emily. "Rudolph the smuggler 'ad a bit of a set-to with excisemen over that on Thursday."

"Well, the other one's not much better."

"That was the 'eadquarters of the underground resistance movement in France for over a week. 'E'd been to one of these 'ere films. 'E was gold-diggin' in South Africa there yesterday, too."

" 'E gets about, doesn't 'e?" said Mr. Heppleback admiringly.

His glance went round the garden again.

"What's 'appened to that tree? It was all right last time I came."

"It may've been one of 'is parachute practices," said Emily, "or it may have been the crash landin' 'e did yesterday."

Mr. Heppleback laughed. "Well, I'll be settin' about my window."

"An' I'll be settin' about my breakfast."

"See you later," said Mr. Heppleback.

"Maybe," said Emily, going back into the hall and closing the door.

If comparative quiet reigned outside, the inside of the Browns' house was less suggestive of peace. Three separate voices called "Emily!" as she turned from the door to go to the kitchen. Emily stood motionless for a few seconds, then, heaving a deep sigh, turned to cope with the situation nearest at hand.

The situation nearest at hand was a good-looking young man of about twenty, standing at the top of the staircase. His face wore an expression of exasperation and a mask of sticky-looking white cream.

"Yes, Mr. Robert?" said Emily, eyeing him dispassionately.

"Where the dickens is my shaving cream?" said Robert.

"In your hand, Mr. Robert," said Emily, in the slow and patient voice in which one points out the obvious.

"This is *shoe* cream!" shouted Robert. "I've got the filthy stuff all over my face."

Emily looked at him, and for a moment—only a moment—the corners of her drooping mouth twitched slightly.

"Well, now," she said, "I do remember your father telling William he shouldn't have his pocket-money unless he kept his shoes cleaner."

"What's that got to do with it?" stormed Robert.

"Well," said Emily, a certain slow enjoyment tempering the despondency of her manner, "I did hear William say that he was going to give them a good clean-up with white cream if he could find any."

"Wait till I get hold of him," said Robert between his teeth, then, twisting his face into lines of agony and making an ineffectual effort to wipe the clinging glutinous substance from his cheeks with his hand, turned and strode back angrily to the bathroom, slamming the door behind him.

"Emily!"

Emily, who was now on her way to the kitchen, stopped.

"Yes, Miss Ethel?"

"Do come up here a minute."

Emily heaved the deep sigh that was her automatic reaction to the never-ceasing demands of fate and went upstairs to the landing, pausing outside the bathroom door to straighten the mat that Robert's volcanic passage had dislodged from its position.

As she reached the landing a bedroom door opened and a girl came out. She was a very pretty girl, with red-gold hair and cornflower-blue eyes, and she wore a rayon dressing-gown that was as near the colour of her eyes as she could get it.

The mirror that she held in her hand showed that she was engaged in the process of "making-up".

"It's kind of you to tidy my room, Emily," she said, "but I wish you wouldn't move things. There were three lipsticks on my dressing-table yesterday, and to-day I can't find one."

"I'm sure I never touched no lipstick, miss," said Emily in a tone of one rebutting a monstrous accusation.

"But lipsticks don't just disappear. Where are they?"

The deadness of Emily's face flickered for a second into life, then went dead again.

"Would you like me to hazard a guess, miss?"

"Yes, if it would get us any nearer my lipsticks."

"You remember William was Big Chief Firewater

all yesterday, and I know he was looking for some war paint."

Ethel stared at her, horror-stricken.

"Emily," she moaned, "you don't mean that my three beautiful lipsticks——"

"It's only a hazard, miss."

The horror in the blue eyes changed to anger.

"That *boy!*" said Ethel.

She turned back into her bedroom, and again the slamming of a door seemed to shake the Browns' house to its foundations.

Emily looked at the slammed door, shrugged her shoulders and turned to go downstairs.

"Emily!"

This time the voice was that of the master of the house, raised on a note of wrath.

Mr. Brown stood at the foot of the staircase. He held a shoe in one hand and a boot-brush in the other.

"Yes, sir?" said Emily.

"Who's covered the boot-brush with shaving cream?" roared Mr. Brown.

"I'm sure I can't think, sir," said Emily.

"This house gets more like a madhouse every day," said Mr. Brown. "Next thing someone'll try to shave with shoe cream."

Again just for a second something seemed to disturb the woodenness of Emily's expression.

"Mr. Robert's already tried it," she said.

"Has he?" said Mr. Brown, and his expression, too, lightened momentarily, as if the mental picture thus summoned afforded him some slight compensation for his own wrongs. Then he resumed his mien of outraged paterfamilias.

"WHO'S COVERED THE BOOT-BRUSH WITH SHAVING CREAM?" ROARED MR. BROWN.

"Send William to me at once," he said sternly.

"He's out, sir," said Emily.

"Out?" said Mr. Brown. "He hasn't had breakfast yet."

"He said he'd be back for that," said Emily.

"What does he mean by going out at this hour?" thundered Mr. Brown. "It's only——" He looked at his watch, and his majestic wrath faded into the testy anxiety of the business man afraid that he'll be late at the office. "It's eight-thirty. Why isn't breakfast ready?"

"It's almost ready, sir," said Emily. "I had a bit of trouble with the refrigerator."

"If I've said it once I've said it a hundred times," said Mr. Brown. "I *must* have breakfast at eight sharp. Can't anyone keep to a schedule in this house? You know perfectly well that if I miss that fast train I have to stop at ten stations on the way to town and——"

Quite suddenly the Browns became too much for Emily. This happened on an average once every three months. She would endure them—and in her heart of hearts adore them—for weeks on end, and then quite suddenly they would become too much for her. Her face worked in an alarming fashion, like something set in motion by a complicated piece of clockwork, and a sound issued like the whirling of rusty wheels.

"All right," she said in a choking voice. "I've slaved for you all ever since Mr. Robert was a baby, but if I don't suit——"

Mr. Brown laid down the shoe and shaving cream on the bottom step and raised his hands in a gesture that expressed sympathy, reassurance and surrender.

"It's all right, Emily. I'm sorry if I spoke hastily.

We appreciate all you do for us more than I can say. It's only that damned slow train. I mean, that slow train. It upsets me for the whole day if I can't have breakfast"—again his voice rose on a note of grievance—"at eight sharp. You understand, don't you?"

"Yes, sir," said Emily almost cheerfully, some deep need of her nature satisfied by the little scene.

Mr. Brown coughed, cleared his throat, picked up his shoe and the shaving cream and retreated to the kitchen.

"Emily!"

The door of the bedroom next to Ethel's had opened and Mrs. Brown emerged.

She was a placid, good-looking woman—with a placidity that had miraculously survived twenty-two years of Mr. Brown and eleven years of William, and with looks that obviously had once held the blue-eyed, red-haired glamour that was now her daughter's.

"Oh, there you are, Emily," she said, as though surprised and pleased to find Emily on the landing, and quite unaware of the little scene she had just overheard. "Everything all right?"

Emily heaved a deep sigh, anxious to erase the memory of the slight sign of cheerfulness she had allowed to escape her.

"As right as it'll ever be in this house, mum," she said dolefully.

Mrs. Brown smiled and let her hand rest for a moment on Emily's shoulder.

"Now, Emily, you know it isn't as bad as all that."

"If you say so, mum," said Emily, in a tone of patient suffering, and added, "Mr. Heppleback's been about the window and the breakfast's nearly ready."

"Good!" said Mrs. Brown, glancing at her watch as she began to go downstairs.

Emily noticed the glance and sniffed as she followed.

"It was the fridge, mum. I couldn't get it open. That fridge 'as never been right since William was at it last week."

"What on earth was he doing with it?"

"He wanted to make an igloo out of ice cubes."

Mrs. Brown laughed. "Never mind, Emily. He goes back to school next week."

Emily's expression of weary resignation intensified. "You never know, mum," she said darkly. "He might catch something."

"Who might catch something?" said Mr. Brown irritably, coming out of the kitchen. "All I want to catch is that fast train."

"All right, dear," said Mrs. Brown. "Breakfast's just ready, isn't it, Emily? Oh, here's Robert. Good morning, Robert."

Robert, spruce and cheerful, all traces of shoe cream removed from his face, was coming downstairs, humming to himself.

"Morning, Mother. Morning, Father."

"Good morning, Robert," said Mr Brown heavily. Then his heaviness lightened. "You shaved with shoe cream, I hear?"

"That's right," said Robert airily. "Hope your shoes enjoyed their shave."

The smile faded from Mr. Brown's face. "I'll have an explanation of this from someone, my boy, or know the reason why," he said.

"Well, we all know who the someone is," said Robert, "and——"

The end of his sentence was drowned by a shattering

salvo on the dinner gong. Emily's state of mind could always be gauged by the way she sounded the dinner gong. On her good days it had a restrained, cheerful note, almost like an old-fashioned musical box. On her bad days it crashed like thunder . . . it held a threat . . . it challenged the whole universe.

"Come along, both of you," said Mrs. Brown, leading the way into the dining-room.

"Morning, Mother," said Ethel, slipping into her seat.

"Good morning, dear."

"Morning, Pop."

Mr. Brown continued to frown at a letter he had just opened.

"Cheer up, Pop," said Ethel, taking her coffee from Mrs. Brown.

"What's this bill for repairing the geyser?" said Mr. Brown. "We only bought the darn thing a month ago."

"It blew up," said Mrs. Brown simply.

"Blew up?" said Mr. Brown, as if the words were unintelligible to him. "How do you mean, blew up?"

"Just blew up," said Mrs. Brown in fuller explanation. "They mended it the same day. I meant to tell you, dear, but I kept put—forgetting."

"The man said it couldn't blow up," said Mr. Brown.

"Well, William heard him say it," said Ethel, "and he tried to prove it."

"In a spirit of pure scientific research," added Robert.

"It wasn't altogether William's fault," said Mrs. Brown.

"It never is, is it?" said Mr. Brown, then, with mounting irritation, "Where *is* the boy? Why doesn't he come in to breakfast? I won't have the place treated as an hotel."

"Eat your breakfast, John dear," said Mrs. Brown. "You'll be missing the late train, too, if you don't hurry."

But the flood of parental wrath was beyond stemming.

"Go and fetch your brother, Robert," said Mr. Brown sternly.

Robert looked up from his bacon with an air of amazed aggrievance. "Me?" he said.

"Yes," said Mr. Brown.

"I haven't had my breakfast, yet."

Mr. Brown's eye became steely. Thunder clouds enveloped his brow.

"Do as your father tells you, Robert dear," said Mrs. Brown hastily. "William's probably in the old barn."

Robert rose with an air of mingled dignity and suffering and went slowly from the room.

Mr. Brown cleared his throat and, in order to tide over the slightly awkward moment, got up from his seat and made his way to the sideboard to cut himself a piece of bread. He had successfully asserted his position as master of his household, but friendly converse immediately after such an assertion is always a little difficult.

"Going to be a fine day," he said, with perhaps over-done heartiness, then, with faint but unmistakable signs of a fresh uprising of irritation: "Where's the bread-knife?"

"Emily," said Mrs. Brown, as Emily entered with a hot-water jug, "you've forgotten the bread-knife."

"No, I haven't," said Emily, in the voice of the

camel receiving the last straw on to its load. "I've
not forgot nothing. It's disappeared. I'm not one to
complain, but——"

"Disappeared?" said Mrs. Brown.

"Nonsense!" said Mr. Brown. "Bread-knives don't
disappear."

"Why not?" put in Ethel. "Lipsticks do."

"We aren't talking about lipsticks, dear," said
Mrs. Brown.

"No, but if William can do away with lipsticks,
he can do the same with bread-knives."

"I think that's very unfair, dear," said Mrs.
Brown. "William isn't responsible for *everything*
that goes wrong in this house."

"Well, if he isn't, it's not for want of trying,"
said Mr. Brown bitterly.

"Now, John dear, do be sensible. What on earth
could William want with a bread-knife?"

Chapter 2

William, the cause of most of the troubles in the Brown household, stood in the old barn, brandishing a bread-knife.

Henry, one of his boon companions, sat on an up-turned packing-case. Douglas, another boon companion, sat on the floor. Ginger, the fourth of the quartet, known collectively as the Outlaws, had not yet arrived.

"Well, then, this man called Arthur," said William, "found the sword called Ex——" He pursued an elusive word through his memory, lost track of it and brought out somewhat uncertainly, "Excelsior. Well, he found this sword called Excelsior stuck in a solid rock. Like this——" He picked up a couple of bricks that lay in a corner of the barn and placed them together) then put the knife between them, its handle protruding. "An' all the others pulled an' pulled an' couldn't get it out an' then this man Arthur came along an'——"

"What did you say the sword was called?" said Douglas.

"Excelsior," said William testily, "an' I wish you wouldn't keep on interruptin'."

"Why?" said Douglas.

"Why, what?" said William.

"Why was it called Excelsior?"

"Well, why shouldn't it be?" said William.

"Why should it be called anything?"

"Well, it *was*," said William. "You're called something, aren't you?"

"Yes," said Douglas, "but I'm a boy, not a sword. Boys *are* called things."

"I thought Excelsior was the name of that man in po'try that carried a strange device over a raging torment," said Henry.

"Look here," said William in a tone of desperation, "are you goin' to let me tell you this story or aren't you?"

"Oh, all right," said Henry. "Go on."

"You might as well call a—call a mincing-machine, Ex—Ex—what you said," said Douglas.

William ignored him. "Well, all the others pulled an' pulled an' pulled an' couldn't get it out."

"You said that before," said Douglas.

"The nex' time you int'rupt—" said William threateningly, then, a note of pathos invading his voice, "You *asked* me to tell you this story, didn't you?"

"We didn't ask you to go on and on sayin' the same thing over an' over again," said Douglas, adding, after a moment's thought, "You might as well call a coal shovel Arthur as a sword."

"The sword wasn't called Arthur," said William. "The *man* was called Arthur. The sword was called Excelsior."

"It must have had the same name as this other man," said Henry. "I know this other man was called Excelsior, 'cause I learnt it once. The shades of night were falling fast an' he met an awful avalanche. I forget the rest, but it was jolly excitin'."

"Gosh!" said William in despair. "Don't you *want* to hear this story?"

"All right," said Henry pacifically. "Go on."

"Well, all the others pulled an' pulled an' couldn't get it out." He turned a quelling eye on Douglas, who had opened his mouth to speak; Douglas, quelled, closed it again. "An' then this man Arthur came along an' pulled it out like this."

William approached the bread-knife in the manner of a boxer approaching his opponent, spat on his hands, seized the handle, made a feint of pulling against tremendous resistance and finally drew it out and brandished it above his head. "Like this!" he repeated. "An' they made him King."

"Why?" said Douglas.

"What d'you mean, why?" said William.

"Why did they make this Excelsior man King?"

"It was *Arthur* they made King, you fathead! They made him King because he pulled this Excelsior thing out."

"It looked easy enough," said Douglas. "I bet I could have done it."

"This other one I learnt about in po'try tried a pass an' ended up by gettin' buried in the snow by dogs,' said Henry. "It's all comin' back to me."

"It's no use trying to tell you int'restin' tales," said William helplessly. "You haven't any *brains*."

"Oh, haven't we?" said Douglas, the light of battle in his eye.

"No, you haven't," said William, accepting the challenge. "If you had any brains, you'd understand an ordin'ry story about a man an' a sword like this. You're bats, both of you, that's what you are."

After an exhilarating scuffle, in which Douglas got

William on to the ground and sat on him, then Henry sat on them both, then they all rolled about the floor and sat on each other, they scrambled to their feet, panting and dishevelled, with amity fully restored.

"Come on," said William. "Let's see what we've brought to eat."

They moved the packing-case on which Henry had been sitting and revealed their improvised larder. Each of the three had left his house before the family breakfast, taking with him such provision as he could lay his hands on, to appease the pangs of early morning hunger. William had purloined from the larder the remains of an apple flan, assuring that amenable organ, his conscience, that it was not large enough to form part of another meal for the whole family and that it was a kindness to his mother to solve the problem of its disposal. Henry had brought half a jar of potted meat ("They're always sayin' it goes bad if you don't use it quick, so we'll use it quick to stop it goin' bad") and Douglas half a loaf ("They were all out to tea yesterday an' they're goin' out to-day an' it's wrong to waste bread so I brought it along"). In addition, they had brought some cold potatoes, a handful of oatmeal, some lemonade powder and a sardine tin, from which the sardines had been removed but which still contained a generous supply of moisture.

"Come on," said William, eyeing the feast with anticipatory relish. "It looks jolly good. Let's start with the apple thing an' spread the potted meat on it to give it more of a taste. Then we can mix the potato an' lemonade powder and sardine juice. I bet *that'll* taste jolly good. It's a jolly sight better than an ordin'ry breakfast. We'll leave the bread to the last."

They sat down on the floor, and William carefully divided the remnant of apple flan into three, spreading each slice thickly with meat paste. They munched happily and in silence for some moments.

"It *is* jolly good," said Henry at last. "I don't know why grown-ups don't mix things more. Funny how they like things dull."

"It's 'cause they're dull themselves," said Douglas indistinctly.

"Well, about this Arthur man," said William (for the trouble with William was that, having once started a subject, he never knew when to stop). "They made him King and he started knights."

"What d'you mean, started nights?" said Douglas. "There've been nights an' days ever since the world began."

"Don't be a chump," said William. "I mean knight spelt with a g, same as gnat and gnaw. He called 'em Knights of the Round Table, an' they went about righting wrongs and rescuing women."

"Oh, I know about *those*," said Henry. "I read about 'em in a book. They brought succour to damsels in distress."

"They may've done that, too," said William vaguely.

A sudden shrill barking cut through the air.

"That's Jumble givin' the alarm," said William, springing to his feet. "Someone's comin'. I bet it's an enemy. Action stations!"

Douglas went to a side window, and Henry, falling on to his stomach, put an eye to a spot in the wall near the ground, where a broken plank afforded a convenient peep-hole.

William peered cautiously out of the barn door, on which hung a crooked notice: "Keep out. Privit."

"Good ole Jumble!" he said approvingly.

Jumble—to ordinary eyes a villainous-looking mongrel but to William's the quintessence of dog perfection—was tied by a piece of rope to a fence, on which hung two notices: "Bewair wotch dog" and "Danger. He Bights." He wagged his stumpy tail in ecstatic acknowledgment of the compliment and, straining hard on his rope, stood on his hind legs, pawing the air in an effort to reach his master.

"Good ole——" began William again, then his jaw dropped open, and he gazed in horror at the figure of a young man striding across the field. "Gosh!" he said, retreating hastily into the barn. "It's Robert! Quick! Put the food away."

He crammed the last of the apple flan into his mouth, and together the three put the loaf, potted meat jar, potatoes and sardine tin under the packing-case. Then they turned to face Robert, who was now framed in the doorway. Robert entered the barn and, ignoring his young brother's friends, looked down at William with an expression of grim disapproval.

"What on earth have you been doing to yourself?" he said.

"Me?" said William innocently, removing the effects of his struggle with Douglas and Henry as best he could by brushing the dust from his suit with his hands and depositing it in his hair as he tried ineffectually to smooth it down.

"Yes, you!" snapped Robert. "And what d'you mean by not coming in to breakfast?"

"Breakfast?" repeated William inanely, playing for time and trying to think of some convincing reason for his absence. "Oh, you mean—breakfast."

"Yes," said Robert impatiently. "Don't make

yourself out more of a half-wit than you are. Not that you could, when one comes to think of it."

"Well, I—I jus' wasn't hungry this mornin', Robert," said William, assuming a not very convincing air of wistfulness, and moving the packing-case with his foot so as to hide a corner of the loaf of bread that was sticking out. "I jus' didn't feel like food. There isn't any lor about people eatin' if they don't feel like it, is there? . . . P'raps"—with a vague and not very hopeful idea of staving off retribution— "p'raps I'm not very well. That's what people do, you know, when they're not very well. They don't feel like food."

"You'd better see the doctor, then," said Robert unsympathetically.

"Oh, no, I'm not ill in that way," said William hastily. "Besides, that doctor never understands my sort of illnesses."

"The trouble is that he does," said Robert dryly. "Anyway, Father says you're to come straight back home to breakfast."

"All right," said William gloomily.

"And what d'you mean by messing about with my shaving cream?"

"That was a mistake, Robert," said William earnestly. "That was jolly annoying for me, too. You see, I wanted some of that white shoe cream an'——"

"Oh, stop talking and come on," said Robert, jerking his head in the direction of the field.

"A' right," muttered William. He untied Jumble's rope, then slowly, draggingly, like a condemned man going to the scaffold, he accompanied Robert across the field, back to the soap and brush, the table napkin and table manners of a despised civilisation.

* * *

William paused in the hall in order to place his cap on the antlered head of a deer that hung on the wall next the hat-stand. It was William's custom to put his cap there, trying different angles to obtain different effects. And as Emily's mood could be gauged from her handling of the dinner gong, so could Mr. Brown's from his reaction to his younger son's cap on the deer's head. There were days when he smiled at it indulgently, there were days when he altered it slightly in order to enhance the effect that William had obviously been aiming at, there were days when he snatched it up with an explosive sound of wrath and flung it on to one of the hat-stand hooks.

To-day, William had not time to do more than draw the peak of his cap down over the bleary glass eyes, imparting a slightly sinister look to the vapid countenance, before he turned his attention to his own person. A glance in the mirror told him that attention was necessary, if not urgent, but an irate "William!" from the dining-room told him at the same time that the process should not be unduly prolonged. He took the clothes-brush from its hook and brushed his hair back from his brow, making it stand up in a circle round his face, removed a few clods of earth from the folds of his stockings, straightened his coat, rubbed a spot of meat paste more firmly into his shirt than it had been before, and entered the dining-room, where Robert was already in his place. Four pairs of eyes met him accusingly as he entered, but he avoided them, assuming the bland innocent air of a boy who has come down in time for breakfast and is surprised to find the rest of the family already assembled.

"Morning, Father," he said with perhaps an excess of politeness, as he took his seat. "Morning, Mother. Morning, Ethel . . ."

"Are you aware," said Mr. Brown portentously, "that you are an hour late for breakfast?"

"I don't know that you can call it an hour, dear," said Mrs. Brown. "We didn't actually start breakfast till after half-past."

"Breakfast in this house," said Mr. Brown, "is timed to start at eight."

"But actually it didn't, dear," said Mrs. Brown.

"It's exactly three minutes past nine now," said Mr. Brown.

"Three and a half," said William, looking at the clock.

"I believe that clock gains," said Ethel.

"It used to lose," said Robert.

"Yes, and then it started gaining. I wish we had an electric clock."

"I repeat," said Mr. Brown impressively, "that breakfast in this house——"

"And you only hear the church clock striking when the wind's in the right direction," said Ethel.

"North," said Robert.

"North-east," said Ethel.

"Well, the church clock isn't much to go by anyway," said Mrs. Brown.

"Will you listen to me for one moment, please?" said Mr. Brown, with an air of patience strained beyond endurance.

"North," said Robert *sotto voce*.

"North-east," said Ethel.

"You're shamefully late for breakfast, William,"

said Mr. Brown, "and I shall deduct a penny from your pocket-money."

"Gosh!" said William with well-simulated horror. Actually he'd expected twopence and was rather relieved.

"Now, look here," said Robert. "This house faces south, doesn't it?"

"South-west," said Ethel.

"South," said Robert.

"The church clock's never been reliable since they found that mouse's nest in it," said Mrs. Brown.

"What did they do with the mouse?" said William.

"One moment," said Mr. Brown. "Will you kindly listen to me, please?"

"Yes, dear," said Mrs. Brown.

"South-west," said Ethel. "You can't deny it gets the evening sun."

"The larder gets the sun all day unfortunately," said Mrs. Brown. "I always think there's something unnatural about those electric clocks."

"Are you listening to me, William?" said Mr. Brown.

"Yes, Father," said William indistinctly.

"And don't talk with your mouth full."

"No, Father," said William, "but it's jolly difficult to know what to do. People say 'answer when you're spoken to' an' 'don't talk with your mouth full', so if you've just got your mouth full when someone asks you something, you've gotter do somethin' wrong. If you wait till you've chewed it all up an' swallowed it before you answer, then you're not answering when you're spoken to and if——"

"*William!*" bellowed Mr. Brown.

"Don't argue with your father, dear," said Mrs.

Brown, "and get on with your breakfast. Pass me the marmalade, will you, Ethel, dear?"

"It is south-west, isn't it?" said Ethel, passing the marmalade.

"It's south, isn't it?" said Robert.

"Probably a little of both, dear," said Mrs. Brown pacifically. "I know that when the wind's in the right direction it dries beautifully."

"What does?" said Robert.

"The wind, dear. Dries clothes on the line. Which reminds me, I must do the laundry directly after breakfast. Don't stick your elbows out like that, William."

"Yes, it almost breaks your ribs sitting next to him," said Ethel. "He needs the whole side of a table to himself."

"He needs a whole room," said Robert.

"A whole house," said Ethel.

"What am I doin' wrong now?" said William with an air of outraged virtue. "I'm jus' sittin' qui'tly eatin' my breakfast."

"Quietly!" groaned Ethel.

"Well, I've got to *chew*, haven't I? I can't swallow things whole. An' I can't help it if my elbows are a diff'rent shape to other people's. You oughter be sorry for me havin' stickin'-out elbows 'stead of goin' on at me about it. I must've been born with stickin'-out elbows, and that's not my fault, is it? You can't help the way you're *born*. At least I never heard you could. It's news to *me* if you can help the way you're born."

He gave a short sarcastic laugh and attacked his fourth piece of bread and marmalade with gusto.

"Now, listen to me, William," said Mr. Brown, doggedly clinging to his position as head of the house and upholder of discipline. "I pass over the disgraceful way you meddled with the shoe cream and shaving cream"—his glance flickered at Robert for a second, but Robert was apparently lost in his own thoughts and unaware of the implication of the flicker—"but I must ask you if you know anything about the disappearance of the bread-knife."

William looked up, and a blank look came over his face.

"The bread-knife?" he said in the wondering tone of one who has never heard of the implement before.

"Yes, the bread-knife," said Mr. Brown. "You know what a bread-knife is, don't you?"

"Oh, that!" said William, playing for time again. "A bread-knife. Yes. I see what you mean now."

"A B-R-E-A-D K-N-I-F-E," spelt Robert.

"That won't convey anything to him," said Ethel. "He probably spells it B-R-E-D N-I-F-E."

"I think his spelling's improving a little," said Mrs. Brown. "He wrote me a very nice letter when I was away at Bognor. On the whole, I mean."

"He spelt 'showers' s-h-a-r-s, didn't he?"

"Well, it's not an easy word," said Mrs. Brown, "and I knew what it meant when I'd said it aloud several times."

"You had good weather there, didn't you, Mother?" said William trailing the red herring across the path without much real hope.

"The bread-knife, William," said Mr. Brown relentlessly.

William, with an effort, retained his look of wondering innocence.

"An implement," explained Ethel, "used for cutting bread."

"And bread, in case you've never heard of it," said Robert, "is a substance compounded of, I believe, flour, water and yeast."

"What's yeast?" said William.

"Yeast," said Robert, "is a substance that ferments sugar."

"Why?" said William.

"I don't know whether it's the yeast that's wrong with it these days," said Mrs. Brown, "but the bread keeps no time at all. I gave the last one back to the baker. It had turned bright green overnight."

"Probably it's the baker that's wrong with it," said Ethel. "He's just got engaged, hasn't he?"

"Yes," said Mrs. Brown. "To that dreadful woman in the post office. I can't think what he sees in her. She was most disagreeable to me over that postal order. I'm sure she dyes her hair."

"She's a terrible gossip," said Ethel. "Some of the things she says are absolute libel."

"Slander," corrected Robert.

"Libel," said Ethel.

"Slander," persisted Robert.

"May I ask you," said Mr. Brown politely, "to give me your attention for a moment. Kindly look at me, William."

William transferred his innocent wondering gaze to his father.

"Are you, or are you not," said Mr. Brown, "responsible for the disappearance of the bread-knife?"

William looked round. There was no escape.

"ARE YOU, OR ARE YOU NOT," SAID MR. BROWN,
"RESPONSIBLE FOR THE DISAPPEARANCE OF THE
BREAD-KNIFE?"

Four pairs of eyes were fixed on him accusingly. Red herrings could no longer serve him. Knitting his brow, he appeared to ponder deeply.

"Come along," said Mr. Brown impatiently. "We haven't got all day."

"Well," said William slowly, with the air of one remembering with difficulty an incident almost hidden by the mists of time, "now I come to think of it, I b'lieve I *did* jus'—jus' borrow it. I didn't think you'd be wantin' it till later. I forgot about breakfast. I didn't think it'd do it any harm jus'—jus' to *use* it. Well, that's what they're made for, isn't it? Knives. To be used, I mean . . ." He looked round the circle again, trying to think of some argument that would postpone the inevitable moment of reckoning, and ended lamely. "Well, if you don't use them, they—they sort of rot, don't they?"

"What exactly have you used that bread-knife for, William?" said Mrs. Brown anxiously.

"I pulled it out of solid rock," said William.

"You *what*?" said Mr Brown.

"Pulled it out of solid rock," said William

"What on earth are you talking about?"

"Well, it was this Excelsior thing. He had to pull it out of solid rock to prove it."

"To prove what?"

"That he was king. And then he started knights."

Mr. Brown considered the explanation in silence for a few minutes, then shrugged helplessly.

"You'll fetch that bread-knife back the minute you've finished your breakfast," he said, "and, if it's damaged beyond repair, you'll pay for a new one out of your pocket-money."

"Yes, Father," said William. "I don't think it's

damaged beyond repair. All the others pulled an' pulled——"

"Get on with your breakfast, dear," said Mrs. Brown.

"The boy's mad, of course," said Ethel.

"Stark, staring," agreed Robert.

"Good lord!" said Mr. Brown, looking at the clock. "I've missed the late train now!"

Chapter 3

"Arise, Sir Douglas," said Henry, tapping the kneeling Douglas sharply on the head with the Browns' bread-knife.

"Gosh! You don't seem to know the difference between knightin' and executin'," said Douglas ruefully, rising to his feet and rubbing his head. "Anyway, I don't think we ought to've started the knight part till William got back. . . . Oh, here he is."

William, having placed Jumble again in his position as watch dog, was just entering the barn.

"Isn't Ginger here yet?" he said, looking round.

"No . . ." said Henry. "Did you get into a row?"

"Not much," said William. "He was mad at first, but I got him to listen to reason. He didn't seem to know anythin' about the Excelsior thing till I told him. Funny he'd never heard of it. Anyway, I've got to take it back. Where is it?"

"It's here," said Henry. "I've jus' been knightin' Douglas with it."

"Well, you've no business to go knightin' people," said William indignantly. "Only the King's allowed to knight people."

"Well, I am the King," said Henry. "I'm King Henry. It's the same as King Arthur, but a diff'rent name."

"You can't be King," said William. "I'm the King and the rest of you's knights."

"Why should you be King?" said Henry, who occasionally made—always unsuccessful—efforts to wrest from William the position of leadership of the gang.

"Well, whose bread-knife is it?" said William, "an' who pulled it out of solid rock?"

"It wasn't solid rock," said Henry. "It was two bricks, an' anyone could have done it. You didn't give anyone else a chance."

Again Jumble's bark cut sharply through the air.

"I bet that's Hubert Lane," said Douglas. "He was watchin' us when we came out this mornin'."

Hubert Lane was the leader of the rival gang of boys and the inveterate enemy of the Outlaws. The feud lent to the daily life of William, Ginger, Henry and Douglas a zest it might otherwise have lacked.

"Action stations!" ordered William. "Can you see who it is, Henry?"

"It's a girl," said Henry, craning his head.

"It isn't even a girl," said William, in a tone of deep disgust, as he peered out of the door. "It's Violet Elizabeth Bott."

Violet Elizabeth was a child of six, with a dominating personality, a ruthless will and a misleadingly winsome expression. She also had a lisp that some people—though not the Outlaws—found engaging. Her chief aim in life was to attach herself to the Outlaws in general and to William in particular, and some uncanny instinct seemed to lead her unerringly to any place where they were.

"I've come to thee you, William," said Violet Elizabeth in explanation of her presence.

"Well, now you've come, you can go away again," said William ungraciously.

"But I don't want to," said Violet Elizabeth sweetly. "I want to thtay here."

"Well, we don't want you," said William.

"That dothn't matter," said Violet Elizabeth forgivingly. "I don't mind."

"Well, we do," said Douglas.

"You don't want to stay with people who don't want you, do you?" said Henry, trying subtler methods.

"Yeth, I do," said Violet Elizabeth serenely. "I want to play Indianth with you. I want to be a thquaw."

"Well, we aren't playing Indians, so go away," said William.

"What are you playing at?" said Violet Elizabeth.

"We're Knights of the Round Table," said William.

"I'll be a Knight of the Round Table, too," said Violet Elizabeth.

"You can't be. Knights were men."

Violet Elizabeth considered. "I'll be a lady knight, then," she said.

"No, you won't," said William, " 'cause there weren't any."

"There would be if I wath one," said Violet Elizabeth simply.

"They were *knights*, I tell you. And knights means *men*. You couldn't do the things knights did, anyway."

"What did they do?" said Violet Elizabeth.

"They went about rescuing damsels in distress," said Henry.

Violet Elizabeth considered this. "I'll be a damthel in dithtreth, then, shall I?" she said, beaming round at them, with the air of one who has solved a difficult problem to the satisfaction of all concerned. "Then you can rethcue me."

"We jolly well don't *want* to rescue you," said William.

"Why not?"

" 'Cause we don't. That's why not."

"That'th no reathon."

"Oh, shut up an' go away."

But Violet Elizabeth was now firmly seated on the packing-case, swinging her short sandalled legs.

"If you haven't got any damthelth in dithtreth to rethcue, you can't be knighth," she said and added: "What *ith* a damthel in dithtreth?"

"Stop talkin' an' go away."

Violet Elizabeth looked at the three stern faces and, seeing no relenting in any of them, decided to use her accustomed weapon.

"I'm going to cry," she said in a choking voice.

"All right," said William. "Go on, cry! We don't care."

Violet Elizabeth fluttered her curling lashes. Her blue eyes swam with tears. Her lips trembled.

"You've made me cry," she said with a heartrending little catch in her voice. The tear-filled eyes and choking voice had melted many a heart in their time, but they didn't melt the Outlaws'.

"Well, get on with it," said William. "Don't take all day over it. Cry, if you're goin' to."

But Violet Elizabeth was too good a tactician to waste her weapons. This one proving useless, she discarded it without further ado. The tears vanished from the blue eyes as suddenly as they had appeared.

"All right," she said in her normal voice, "if you won't let me be a lady knight, I'll thcream an' I'll thcream an' I'll thcream, till I'm thick—an' I *can*," she ended proudly.

They looked at her, nonplussed. They knew that she could. She had often proved her prowess in that field.

"We'd better let her, William," said Henry. "If she starts screamin' someone'll hear an' come along an' make a row. They always do."

"Oh, all right," muttered William.

"Can I be a lady knight, William?" said Violet Elizabeth eagerly.

"Yes," said William disgustedly, "but we jolly well don't want you. Remember that!"

"Yeth, I will, William," said Violet Elizabeth happily. She clapped her hands and began to dance about the floor of the barn. "I'm a lady knight! I'm a lady knight! I'm a lady knight!"

William watched her, scowling morosely, his hands dug deeply into his pockets.

"Gosh!" he said. "The minute you let that girl into anything, it's all messed up."

Suddenly Douglas, who was standing near the door, gave a shout.

"Look who's coming down the lane," he said.

William and Henry ran to join him in the doorway. Down the lane that bordered the field sailed an exultant figure on a bicycle with a pair of boxing gloves round its neck.

"It's *Ginger*!" said William.

"On a *bicycle*!" said Henry.

The figure turned in at the open gate and made its way across the field towards the old barn. Then, in an excess of self-confidence and exultation, it took its hands from the handle-bars and zigzagged wildly towards the open doorway. There was a shout, a crash, a burst of frantic barking from Jumble, and the bicycle and its rider rolled to the ground, lying there several feet apart.

William, Henry and Douglas ran to pick up the bicycle.

"Gosh, it's a beauty!" said William, examining it.

"The mudguard's a bit bent," said Douglas, "but that's all."

"You are an idiot," said Henry to the still recumbent figure of Ginger. "You might have smashed the whole thing."

Ginger sat up and rubbed his ankle.

"I might be dead for all you seem to care," he said bitterly.

"Well, you deserve to be," said William. "Fooling about with a bike like this!"

They continued to examine the bicycle and ignore Ginger.

"It's got a three-speed gear," said Douglas.

"And look at these boxing gloves," said Henry, picking them up from the grass.

"Look at its tyres."

"I b'lieve I've broken my neck," said Ginger, rising painfully to his feet.

"Well, the bike isn't broken, an' that's all that matters," said William.

Ginger limped up to them and grabbed the handle-bars.

"You leave it alone."

"Whose is it?" said William.

"It's mine," said Ginger. He grabbed the boxing gloves from Henry. "Those are mine, too."

"You'll get in a row when someone finds you've taken them," said Henry.

"I tell you, they're mine. Hector gave them me."

"Hector?" echoed the others.

Hector was Ginger's elder brother, and such gifts from elder brothers were unknown in their experience.

"Is he dyin'?" said Douglas with interest. "I once read a tale about a man what was dyin' an' he gave all his things away an' then he got better an' wanted them back."

"No, he's gettin' married," said Ginger.

"But why's he given you them?"

"Someone's givin' him a motor bike for a weddin' present, so he doesn't want an ole push bike."

"An' what about the boxing gloves?" said William.

"She doesn't like vi'lence."

"Who doesn't?"

"The girl he's marryin'. She says boxing's barb'rous."

"What's that?"

"It's same as bein' a savage. He's got to give up rugger, too, 'cause she says that's barb'rous, too."

"She can't know much about savages if she thinks they box an' play rugger. She mus' be a jolly ign'rant girl."

"Yes, she is. She doesn't take any int'rest in anythin' sensible. She wasn't even int'rested in that dead rat we found, and it was a smashin' one."

"Gosh, yes, it was. Well, I'd jolly well rather be barb'rous than be same as what she is."

"Fancy people *marryin'* 'em!" said William in disgust.

"When's he goin' to get married?" said Henry.

"When they can find a house," said Ginger. "There aren't enough houses yet."

"There's houses all over the place," said Douglas.

"Yes, but people are livin' in 'em."

"Come on," said William. "Let's take the bike into the barn."

They entered the barn, pushing the bicycle and carrying the boxing gloves.

"Hello, Ginger," said Violet Elizabeth. "You did make a futh about falling off your bithycle. I onth," proudly, "thaw a *real* acthident with real blood and an amblanth."

"What's *she* doin' here?" said Ginger disgustedly to William.

"I'm a lady knight," said Violet Elizabeth importantly. "I rethcue damthonth."

"Damsons!" jeered William.

"You thaid damthonth."

"I didn't."

"What did you thay, then?"

"I shan't tell you."

"You *did* thay damthonth," said Violet Elizabeth with quiet confidence.

"What are you talking about?" said Ginger.

"Well, we're Knights of the Round Table," said William. He looked at the packing-case. "Tell you what! We'll have that for the table an' it's square, so we'll be Knights of the Square Table." He pushed Violet Elizabeth unceremoniously from her perch. "And they didn't sit on it, either."

"I don't think much of their mannerth," said Violet Elizabeth severely, as she picked herself up. "Puthing people off tableth!"

"We're going to do the same as they did," said

Henry, ignoring her, "go about righting wrongs."

"What sort of wrongs did they right?" asked Ginger.

"Well," vaguely, "people bein' put in dungeons an' that sort of thing."

"And puthed off tableth," said Violet Elizabeth.

Again they ignored her.

"Come on," said William. "Let's sit round the table and have a meeting. An' *you* needn't come, Violet Elizabeth."

They took their seats on the floor round the packing-case.

"I'm going to come," said Violet Elizabeth, inserting her small person between Henry and Douglas. "I'm a lady knight and lady knighth *did* come."

"Let's take no notice of her," said William. "Now in a meeting there's got to be a President an' a Secretary and Treasurer. I know that, 'cause Robert's Treasurer of the cricket club. The President's the most important, an' it's a jolly difficult thing to be, 'cause Robert says there's always some jackass at the meeting who tries to put spokes in the wheels."

"Why?" said Douglas.

"Oh, shut up."

"Can I be the preth'dent, William?" said Violet Elizabeth.

"No."

"Can I be the thecretary, then?"

"No!"

"Can I be the treatherer?"

"*No*."

Violet Elizabeth considered.

"I'll have to be the jackath, then."

"You're that, all right!" said William, guffawing at his own wit.

"What *ith* a jackath?" said Violet Elizabeth.

"You ought to know," said William.

"What did you thay it did at the meeting?"

"It kept quiet."

"Oh," said Violet Elizabeth.

"Come on, let's get on with it," said Ginger impatiently.

"Who'll be the president?" said Henry. "Shall I be it?"

"No. I'll be it," said Ginger. "I've got a bicycle."

"That doesn't make any diff'rence," said Douglas. "I've got a concertina. At least I had till my father took it off me, 'cause they made such a fuss next door."

"I'm the president," said William shortly.

"All right," agreed the others.

They hadn't had any real hope that anyone but William would be president.

"What does the president do?" said Ginger.

"He tells them what to talk about."

"That's rot," said Henry. "We've got to talk about righting wrongs."

"You've got to talk about what I tell you to talk about if I'm the president," said William. "If I tell you to talk about—about *saucepans*, you've got to talk about 'em."

"What do you want to talk about thauthpanth for?" said Violet Elizabeth.

"I don't," said William testily.

"You jutht thaid you did."

"I did *not*."

"I think ith thilly," said Violet Elizabeth. "All thith futh about knighth and rethcuing damthonth juth to talk about thauthpanth."

"Shut up," said William irritably. Then, to the others, "Now, we've got to find some wrongs an'——"

"What have thauthpanth got to do with it, anyway?" demanded Violet Elizabeth passionately.

"I wish you'd shut *up*," said William in exasperation. "I never said they'd got anything to do with anything."

"Yeth, you did, you thaid——"

"If—you—don't—keep—quiet, we'll throw you out."

"All right," said Violet Elizabeth, relapsing into temporary obscurity.

"Now listen, varlets," said William, speaking quickly in an attempt to get through as much business as possible before Violet Elizabeth could rally her forces.

"Thought we were knights," said Douglas.

"You are. Varlet is another word for them. Now listen. The first thing to do is to swear by Excelsior not to tell anyone about us bein' Knights of the Square Table. If Hubert Lane and his gang got to know about it, they'd try to mess it all up, so——" He looked round. "Where's that bread-knife? Gosh! I ought to've taken it home. Never mind. I'll take it when we've finished. Here it is. Now you've all got to touch it, an' that means you've sworn an oath to keep it secret."

One by one, with expressions of deep solemnity, they laid a finger on the blade of the bread-knife, as it was handed to each by William.

"We've got a bigger bread-knife than that at home," said Violet Elizabeth in a tone of superiority. "Ith got little thpiketh on."

They ignored her.

"Now," said William, "what wrongs shall we start rightin' first?"

ONE BY ONE, WITH EXPRESSIONS OF DEEP SOLEMNITY,
THEY LAID A FINGER ON THE BLADE OF THE BREAD-
KNIFE.

"My father's got a lot of wrongs," said Ginger. "Income tax an' rates an' the man next door's dog scratchin' up his plants."

"We can't bother with things like that," said William. "It'd take *months* to put those right. We'll start on somethin' a bit smaller than those."

"What about startin' on ole Markie?" said Henry. "We've got enough wrongs from *him*. Keepin' people in's the same as throwin' them into dungeons, an' he's always keepin' us in."

"Oh, I dunno about that," said William evasively. His dealings with his headmaster had never been such as to make him desire any further acquaintance. "I think we'd better leave ole Markie alone. My father says he does his best."

"He does his best to make our lives a misery, all right," said Henry morosely. "Gosh! When I think of the way he went on jus' 'cause my mouse got out of my pocket——"

"Well, never mind ole Markie," said William. "There's more important wrongs than ole Markie."

"There's penshuns," said Ginger.

"What d'you mean, penshuns?" said William.

"Well, the mean way they give penshuns to ole people jus' for bein' ole an' won't give 'em to young people jus' for bein' young."

"We tried to get penshuns for boys once," William reminded him, "but it didn't come off."

"I've got a thecret," said Violet Elizabeth suddenly.

They looked at her. Her small face wore an expression of such deep satisfaction that their curiosity was aroused, despite themselves.

"What d'you mean, you've got a secret?" said William.

"I mean, I've got a thecret," said Violet Elizabeth.

"What sort of a secret?"

"A *thpethial* thecret," said Violet Elizabeth, "and I than't tell it you."

"Well, we aren't interested in your old secret, anyway," said William, turning to Ginger as if in dismissal of the subject. He looked at Ginger absently for a few moments, then turned back to Violet Elizabeth. "What's it about?"

"I than't tell you."

"That's a good thing," said William, " 'cause we don't want to know."

"You would if you knew what it wath," said Violet Elizabeth.

"That's a batty thing to say," said William. He moved his shoulders so as to exclude her from the conference. "Now let's get on with this wrong-rightin'."

"Ith a terribly *exthiting* thecret," said Violet Elizabeth.

"You needn't go on talkin', 'cause we're not listenin' to you," said William loftily.

"Is it something to do with us?" said Ginger.

"Yeth," said Violet Elizabeth, a smile of lingering relish on her lips. "Yeth, it *ith* thomething to do with you. An' I than't tell you what it ith."

"Well, we don't want to know, so you can shut up," said William. "Now about this wrong . . ."

They discussed the general question of righting wrongs for some minutes, but they discussed it in a desultory half-hearted fashion, throwing covert glances at Violet Elizabeth as they did so. There was still that look of secret satisfaction on her face, that smile of relish on her lips. . . .

"If you knew my thecret," she said, "you wouldn't be juth thitting there an' *talking*."

William turned to her with an air of amused indulgence.

"All right," he said, "you can tell us it, if you like."

"I don't want to," said Violet Elizabeth.

"Why?" said Douglas.

" 'Cauth you've been tho nathty to me. You've all been nathty to me all morning. If you'll thay you're thorry you've been nathty to me, I'll tell you my thecret."

"If you think," said William sternly, "that we're goin' to say we're sorry to a silly kid like you, you're jolly well mistaken."

"All right," said Violet Elizabeth sweetly. "Then I won't tell you my thecret."

"Don't, then," said William and returned to the discussion.

But somehow the life had gone out of it. After a few moments he turned again to Violet Elizabeth. "If your secret's worth us sayin' we're sorry, we're sorry, but, if it turns out not to be, we take it back and we're not sorry," he offered.

"All right," said Violet Elizabeth, accepting the compromise.

"What is it, then?"

"I can thee Hubert Lane."

"*What?*"

"He'th looking through the window."

Four pairs of eyes wheeled round to meet the fat pallid face of Hubert Lane gazing through the dusty window of the barn.

They sprang to their feet.

"*Gosh!*" said William.

"I thaid it wath a *thpethial* thecret," said Violet Elizabeth triumphantly.

Chapter 4

Hubert sat on the packing-case in the old barn. He had been gagged by Ginger with William's none-too-clean handkerchief and bound by William with Jumble's rope.

The chase had been long and exciting, and at one point Hubert had successfully eluded them by clambering on to a haystack, but he had leaned too far over the edge to watch his departing pursuers, over-balanced and fallen to the ground, attracting their attention by his yell of fright and pain.

After that he had been secured and marched smartly back to the old barn.

The four Outlaws stood in a circle around him. Jumble, who seemed to consider himself solely responsible for the capture—though in reality he had considerably hampered it by giving away the position of the Outlaws at every turn and getting mixed up with William's feet as he finally grabbed his prey—sat in front of Hubert with his tongue hanging out of his mouth and his tail thumping the ground triumphantly.

Violet Elizabeth, who had tried to join the circle of Outlaws but had been resolutely ejected from it by their elbows at whatever point she appeared, stood in the background watching the proceedings with a mixture of horror and delight.

"You're a spy, Hubert Lane," said William sternly, "an' you know what they do to spies."

"They shoot 'em," supplemented Ginger.

Hubert freed himself from William's none-too-clean handkerchief by the simple process of jerking his head to one side, causing the cloth to fall limply round his neck.

"Well, you aren't much of a gagger," said William indignantly to Ginger. "Look at it! Came off as easy as easy. Nice mess we'd be in if it was a real war, an' you weren't a better gagger than that."

"It was a rotten gag," said Ginger.

"It was a jolly good handkerchief," said William, retrieving it. "My aunt gave it me las' Christmas."

"It was all right before you tore that piece off yesterday to carry your tadpoles in."

"Well, I had to carry them in somethin', hadn't I?" William justified himself. "They can't walk, can they? It's news to *me* that tadpoles can walk. An' I wanted the rest of the handkerchief to carry the newt in. I wanted to carry them sep'rately, 'cause I didn't want the tadpoles to eat it."

"Tadpoles don't eat newts."

"They do."

"They don't. Tadpoles eat each other. They go one less every day. I know, 'cause——"

"Oh, get on with the spy business," said Henry impatiently, for it was well known that, when once William and Ginger started an argument, they could carry it on indefinitely.

"A'right," said William, turning back to the subject in hand.

The subject in hand, who had been gurgling and

"YOU'RE A SPY, HUBERT LANE," SAID WILLIAM
STERNLY, "AN' YOU KNOW WHAT THEY DO TO SPIES."

spluttering during William's and Ginger's conversation, at last found its voice.

"If you shoot me," he said on a high-pitched note of terror, "I'll tell my father."

"We ought to search him first," said Ginger. "That's what they do with real spies. They search 'em to see if they've got any 'criminating documents."

"All right," said William, "let's search him."

Hubert's pockets were disappointing. They did not even contain the miscellaneous assortment of oddments that one expects to find in a schoolboy's pockets. They contained a clean handkerchief, neatly folded, a diary in which he recorded the marks he obtained from his lessons and occasionally the salient point of knowledge he had gained in each, a book of stamps and a letter from his godmother beginning, "Dear Hubert, I am glad to learn from you what good progress you are making at school——"

"I bet that's 'criminating," said Ginger. "I bet it's a code."

"It's not worth anythin' to anyone, anyway," said William.

"What'll we do with him now?" said Henry.

"We've got to find out his military secrets."

"How?"

"Torcher him," said Violet Elizabeth shrilly from the background.

"Shut up," said William. "Where's Excelsior? Gosh! I ought to've taken it back. I will after this."

He picked up the bread-knife from the floor and approached Hubert with it. Hubert's pallid countenance took on a greenish tinge.

"You'll catch it, William Brown, if you touch me with that bread-knife. I'll tell my father."

"Pull hith teeth out," said Violet Elizabeth.

"It isn't a bread-knife. It's Excelsior," said William.

"Thtick pinth into him," said Violet Elizabeth.

"What were you doin', spyin' on us?" said William to Hubert.

Hubert's face had resumed its normal pallor as he saw that the bread-knife was not to be put to any immediate use. "You wouldn't mind people lookin' at you if you weren't doing something wrong," he said.

"Pull hith hair," said Violet Elizabeth.

"We'll pull yours if you don't shut up," said William. "Now look here, Hubert Lane," assuming his most impressive manner. "You're a spy an' you've been caught spyin' an' condemned to death, but if you'll swear by Excelsior never to reveal any secrets that you've heard . . . Here! Where's that bread-knife? Violet Elizabeth, put that bread-knife down."

"No, I won't," said Violet Elizabeth, dodging William's avenging figure round the barn. "You've not let me *tutch* it yet. I'm going to have the Exthelthior and I'm goin' to be *queen*. I told you the thecret an' I'm goin' to be *queen*."

"You jolly well can't be," panted William. "Catch her, Ginger. I pulled it out of solid rock an' it's our bread-knife, anyway, an'——"

"*I* could pull it out of tholid rock, too," said Violet Elizabeth. "An' ith a rotten bread-knife. It hathn't got little thpiketh on ith edge like ourth hath an'——"

"Get her, Henry!"

In the scuffle that preceded the securing of Violet Elizabeth, William sustained a cut chin, Henry a bitten finger and Ginger a long scratch down his cheek. Douglas, who belonged to the school of thought that considers discretion the better part of valour, had hovered on the outskirts of the group, but even he had an ominous dark patch on his forehead, where the handle of the knife had caught him when Violet Elizabeth, seeing capture inevitable, had flung it clear of the skirmish.

"Well, now—" said William, brandishing his retrieved weapon, and looking round for his captive. Then his jaw dropped and he gaped about him in consternation. The captive was not there. Hubert had taken advantage of their momentary preoccupation to undo the not very secure knots of the rope and make a bolt for freedom. They ran to the door and looked round the empty countryside.

"Gosh! he's got away," said William. "That's your fault, Violet Elizabeth."

"No, it ithn't," said Violet Elizabeth with spirit. "Ith yourth. You've all been very nathty to me an' I wouldn't be queen now if you *athked* me to an' I don't *want* your nathty old bread-knife an' you didn't pull it out of tholid rock, 'cauth I've *theen* it at your houthe when I've been to tea an' all I've theen you pull it out of ith tholid *bread*, an' you're nathty rough boyth an' you've pulled my hair ribbon off an' I'm glad Hubert Lane got away an' I'm glad I thcratched you an' bit you and I with I'd bit you more an' I'm goin' home now an' I'm not going to thay good-bye to you, tho there!"

With that, Violet Elizabeth, tousled head held high, strode lightly out of the barn into the sunshine.

William was the first to rally his forces.

"Yes, an' you can jolly well stay away," he shouted, feeling the come-back a little weak but better than none at all.

Douglas was leaning against the doorpost, tenderly caressing his bruise. "Gosh, it might have ended in death," he said.

Then William had another idea. Violet Elizabeth was almost out of hearing, but he had a good carrying voice.

"An' we take back that 'sorry'," he bellowed.

Violet Elizabeth's answer was to turn round, put out a small pink tongue, then proceed lightly and nonchalantly on her way.

"Good riddance to bad rubbish!" called Ginger.

"Black beetles, sixpence a bottle!" called Henry, in reference to the supposed ingredients of the Digestive Sauce manufactured by Violet Elizabeth's father, but, if either of these flowers of rhetoric reached Violet Elizabeth, she gave no signs of having heard them.

The Outlaws turned somewhat dejectedly to consider the immediate situation.

"Well, Hubert's gone," said William. "We can't catch him now."

"I bet I could," said Henry. "I could take Ginger's bike and catch him in no time."

"Oh, could you?" said Ginger indignantly, "an' I could catch you in no time."

"Well, if a knight's got to go an' capture someone, he ought to be able to ride out on a bike."

"Whose bike is it?" said Ginger.

"Well, we're all knights, aren't we?" said Douglas. "We oughter *share* things."

"You're thinking of communists," said Ginger. "It's communists that share things, not knights."

"My father goes to shareholders' meetings," said Henry a little vaguely.

"Well, he's a communist, then," said Ginger, "but

I bet he doesn't let you ride his bike, does he?"

"No," said Henry.

"Well, then," said Ginger triumphantly, "that *proves* it."

They looked impressed but a little bewildered by this logic.

"I've got an idea," said William suddenly. "I've been thinkin' an' I've got an idea."

They turned to him eagerly. William's ideas generally had that quality of the unexpected that adds a zest to life.

"Yes?" they said.

"We'll all get bikes," said William.

"How?" they chorused.

"Well, listen," said William. "Ginger got his bike 'cause his brother was gettin' married, didn't he?"

"Yes."

"Well," said William, "we've all got grown-up brothers, haven't we?"

"Yes."

"Well, we'll get 'em all married. Then we'll all get bikes."

There was such calm assurance in William's manner that just for a moment Henry and Douglas almost felt the hard circle of the handle-bars between their fingers. . . . Then they came down to earth.

"It's not as easy as all that," said Henry.

"That's right," said William sarcastically. "Start making objections. There's me wearin' out my brain thinkin' out a good idea to get us all bikes, an' all you can do is to make objections."

"I only said it wasn't as easy as all that," said Henry, "and it isn't."

"Doesn't even sound *poss'ble* to me," said Douglas,

frowning thoughtfully. "You can't get people married jus' 'cause you want their bikes. If you could, everyone'd be married an' everyone'd have bikes."

"Oh, shut up arguin'," said William. "How d'you think things'd've got done in hist'ry, if people kept on arguin' an' making objections like you?"

"Some things didn't get done in hist'ry," said Douglas. "I could tell you lots of things that_didn't get done in hist'ry."

"Well, we don't want to hear 'em," said William. "I bet you don't know 'em, anyway. I bet I know more hist'ry than what you do."

"I bet you don't," said Douglas.

"I bet I do."

"I bet you don't. What did your hist'ry report say last term?"

"Well, never mind that now," said William evasively. "I know that things like the Magna Corpus Act an' that man Wolsey getting made a cardigan wouldn't 've happened if everyone'd kept arguin' an' sayin' they couldn't get their brothers married."

"Cardinal," said Henry.

"Well, that's what I said, isn't it?" said William pugnaciously.

"No, it isn't," said Henry.

"What's all this got to do with rightin' wrongs?" said Ginger, who, as the sole possessor of a bicycle, had preserved a certain air of detachment throughout the discussion.

"It's got a jolly lot to do with rightin' wrongs," said William. "You've got a bike an' we haven't an' that's a jolly big wrong an' we're goin' to right it."

"Well, you oughter right other people's wrongs, not your own," said Ginger virtuously.

"S'all very well for you," said William. "You've *got* a bike. . . . All right, we'll right other people's wrongs, too. I don't mind how many wrongs I right, once I get started. I bet they'll be comin' to us from all over the world," he went on, giving rein to his ever-glorious optimism, "once they know about us rightin' wrongs."

"How'll they get to know?" said Douglas.

"We'll put up a notice," said William after a moment's thought. "I'm jolly good at notices."

"I think we ought to charge for it," said Henry. "I mean, they have to pay for havin' their windows mended an' their chimneys swept, so I think they ought to pay for havin' their wrongs righted. I don't think it's fair to the people who mend windows an' sweep chimneys if we right wrongs for nothin'."

"Did the real knights charge?" said Douglas.

"I bet they did," said William. "I bet they had a notice stuck on the door same as we're goin' to have an' made everyone pay. Well, let's make the notice now."

It was decided to go to Ginger's house to make the notice, as his house was nearest the old barn and there was a tin of red paint on his garage shelf.

They secured the paint as unostentatiously as possible and went up to Ginger's bedroom, where their efforts took a good half-hour, nearly the whole tin of red paint and seven pages of Ginger's arithmetic exercise book.

The lettering was traced on to the pages with the end of Ginger's pen-holder, dipped in the tin of red paint. Both design and spelling were erratic, but to the Outlaws it represented the highest achievement of art.

GNITES OF THE SQUARE TABLE

RONGS WRIGHTED

SMALL RONGS, 6*d*.

BIG RONGS, 1*s*.

PLEASE GNOCK

Only Douglas was a little doubtful about it—and that on commercial rather than artistic grounds.

"I don't think anyone'll pay all that money jus' to get a wrong righted," he said. "It's not worth it."

"It jolly well is," said William indignantly. "People in hist'ry paid *pounds* to get wrongs righted. It's jolly cheap, isn't it, Ginger?"

"Yes," said Ginger.

He spoke a little absently. He was noticing for the first time the devastation that surrounded him.

The red paint had spread like a sea all over his homework table, and bright splashes adorned rug, carpet and even the fireplace surround.

"I say!" he went on nervously. "It's made a bit of a mess, hasn't it? *Gosh!* Look at the carpet."

"We'll clear it up," William assured him, taking out his handkerchief and beginning to rub the spots on the carpet.

"Hi! You're only makin' a big mess instead of a lot of little ones," said Ginger.

"Well, I'm tryin' to help, aren't I?" said William aggrievedly. "I'm doin' my best."

"It's too small, that handkerchief of yours," said Douglas, taking the bath towel from Ginger's towel rail and setting to work on the table.

"I say! Mind what you're doin' to that towel," said Ginger, whose visions of maternal wrath were gaining each moment in vividness and power.

"They wash, towels do," said Douglas carelessly. "That's what they send 'em to the laundry for, isn't it? If a laundry can't wash a bit of paint out of a towel, it's not much good."

Henry had chosen a somewhat simpler method and was taking spots of paint from the tiled surround of the fireplace with his finger and wiping it on his stockings.

William, having discarded his handkerchief, was trying the effect of Ginger's sponge on the paint-sodden table.

"Oh, come on," said Ginger, looking round with rising apprehension, "let's get away before they come and find it. They'll make a jolly big fuss when they *do* find it, but, if I'm not here, they can't do anything to me till I am."

Impressed by the force of this argument, the Outlaws took up the notice, and, creeping soundlessly down the staircase, slipped out of the side door.

"Yes, it's a jolly good notice," said William, when he had fixed it to the door of the old barn with a rusty nail that he had found on the floor and hammered it in with his shoe. Then he looked round the barn again. In the centre of the floor lay the bread-knife, its blade gleaming in the sunshine.

"Gosh!" he said, conscience-stricken. "There's Excelsior! I've not taken it back yet. Come on. I'll get in another row if it's not back by lunch-time."

"What about the people that want wrongs righted?" said Ginger.

"They'll have to wait," said William. "If we're

goin' to right their wrongs for them, surely they can do a little thing like waitin' a few minutes."

"They might be in a hurry," said Douglas, "an' we don't want to miss any good wrongs. Let's tell them to leave a note."

"All right," said William. "Anyone got a pencil?"

Henry had one. There was no point to it, and none of the Outlaws had penknives with them, so William chewed at it till a piece of lead was visible and then scribbled at the bottom of the notice:

"If out leeve noat."

"Pity we couldn't do it in red like the rest," he said, gazing at it critically. "Still, it can't be helped, an' we'll be back again soon. Come on."

They set off briskly across the fields, Ginger wheeling his bicycle and Jumble trotting beside them.

"Funny taste that red paint of Ginger's has," said Henry, who had been licking the paint from his fingers with the vague idea of tidying himself up before returning to civilisation.

"They nearly all taste the same," said William. "Once we had some green paint that tasted a bit diff'rent. Once," with modest pride, "I was axshally *sick* with paint."

"My mother's given Hector a wooden seat for his garden when he gets married," said Ginger, "an' he's paintin' it yellow. I keep tryin' to help him, but he won't let me."

"What about this gettin' *our* brothers married?" demanded Douglas. "We've been forgettin' about that."

"Oh, yes," said William, "we've got to fix that up. It's quite easy. I've got a jolly good idea. What girl is your brother keen on?"

"I've forgotten," said Douglas. "It's a diff'rent one each week."

"Well, find out which it is this week," said William.

"And what then?" said Henry.

"Listen an' I'll tell you," said William.

They listened in silence while William unfolded his plan.

"Yes," said Henry judicially when he had finished, "it's a jolly good idea."

"I always have jolly good ideas," said William complacently, adding hastily, as he saw three mouths opening to offer proof of the contrary: "Well, the ideas are all right, but people sometimes mess them up." They had reached the gate of William's house now. "Here we are. Wait for me while I take the bread-knife in."

They waited in a group by the gate while William, with an elaborate display of secrecy (for he was pretending that he was a Secret Service agent entering a spy's house in order to steal back some stolen papers), crept round several bushes on the lawn, then, with coat collar turned up and the bread-knife held at a threatening angle, sidled into the house by the open front door.

The hall was empty. The dining-room was empty. The fingers of the hall clock stood at twelve o'clock. He put the knife on the sideboard and returned to the three at the gate.

"I say," he said, "we've got a whole hour before lunch. What'll we do?"

"We ought to go back to see if anyone's brought

any wrongs to be righted," said Douglas, who was always the most conscientious of the four.

"No, I'm sick of rightin' people's wrongs," said William.

"You haven't righted any yet," Henry reminded him.

"All right. I never said I had," said William. "I mean, I'm sick of thinkin' about it. Let's do somethin' else this morning, an' go back to rightin' wrongs this afternoon."

"What shall we do?"

"Let's go to the tadpole pond at the Manor," said William.

Chapter 5

William ran back into the house to fetch an empty jam jar for the tadpoles, and then the four of them made their way down the road towards the Manor.

They employed their usual means of procedure—a means that combined the maximum of activity with the minimum of progress—kicking stones across the road, delving into the ditches that bordered the road in search of real or imaginary water rats, stopping occasionally to indulge in friendly scuffles and wrestling matches.

Ginger had left his bicycle at William's house, using various complicated devices for its safety. Not only had he locked the padlock that Hector had given him with the bicycle, but he had also tied it to the garage door with Mrs. Brown's clothes-line and rigged up an elaborate "burglar" trap that involved the use of the alarm clock from Robert's bedroom and the "lead" of Mrs. Brown's electric iron. Test of this invention had given negative results, but Ginger had not lost faith in it. Not content with this, they had left Jumble on guard, wearing his misleading notice, "Danger. He Bights." Even so, Ginger's mind was not wholly at ease.

"If anyone takes it," he said, "I'm goin' to write to Scotland Yard. The p'liceman here isn't any good. He just wastes his time interferin' with people what aren't doin' any harm 'stead of catchin' thieves. I don't think he knows how to catch a thief. I don't think he's ever been *taught*. He's not likely to catch any murderers, either, 'cause he's a murderer himself."

Ginger spoke bitterly, having been caught by the youngest member of the local police force in the act of entering the vicar's hen-run, in search of feathers for his Red Indian head-dress, and soundly cuffed only the day before.

"It won't be any use writing to Scotland Yard," said William. "I wrote once, an' they didn't even answer."

"Well, you wrote sayin' you wanted to be a detective," Douglas reminded him, "an' p'raps they'd got enough detectives."

"I'd make a jolly good detective," said William. "When I went out in that beard of Robert's with a corked moustache an' lines on my face, no one knew who I was. Well, hardly anyone."

"Well, Scotland Yard didn't want you, anyway."

"No," agreed William gloomily, "but I think it was jolly rude not to answer. The War Office is jolly rude, too. I wrote to it twice an' it never answered."

"P'raps they didn't want any more gen'rals," said Henry.

"Well, I said I'd be a drummer boy, if they'd got enough gen'rals," said William. "I once read a story about a drummer boy that rose to be a general."

"William!"

They turned to see Violet Elizabeth following them down the road. She looked wistful and appealing. William scowled at her fiercely.

"If you think," he said, "that we're goin' to have anythin' more to do with *you* after this mornin'——"

"Thith morning?" said Violet Elizabeth wonderingly, as if wholly unaware of his meaning.

"Yes, this morning," said William sternly, turning to proceed on his way.

Violet Elizabeth continued to follow them.

"I don't see how I'm ever goin' to get to be Prime Minister or Head of Scotland Yard or Commander-in-Chief if they won't even let me *start*," said William, who was occasionally slightly worried about his prospects.

"I should think bein' Prime Minster's a bit dull," said Ginger. "They don't have to do anythin' but make speeches."

"I'm jolly good at makin' speeches," said William.

But the discussion had become somewhat half-hearted. They were all uncomfortably aware of Violet Elizabeth following silently in their tracks.

"Anyway, you could get someone else to write 'em for you," said Henry. "Some people are *trained* writin' speeches. They pass exams in it."

"I still think a chimney sweep's more fun," said Douglas.

"William!"

They ignored her.

"William, I'm thorry."

They still ignored her.

"Or an animal shop," said Ginger.

"William." There was a note of reproach in her voice. "William, I've *thaid* I'm thorry."

"You'd jolly well better be, too," growled William.

"Where are you going, William?" said Violet Elizabeth, encouraged by even this response.

"I shan't tell you."

"I can find out."

"No, you can't."

"Yeth, I can!" said Violet Elizabeth, who was already recovering something of her usual aplomb. "I can juth walk along the road after you like thith and go wherever you go. You can't thtop people walkin' along the road after you."

"Well, we're not goin' to take any notice of you," said William. "We're not goin' to say a single word to you, so there!"

He turned again to continue his conversation with the other three.

"Or an ice-cream cart," said Henry.

"I jolly well wouldn't sell any of my ice-creams, if I had an ice-cream cart," said William. "I'd eat 'em all myself."

"William!"

They ignored her.

"William, I've got thome thweeth."

"I'm not int'rested in your rotten ole sweets," said William. He paused for a moment and added, "What sort are they?"

"Mint, William."

"Well, I don't care whether they're mint or not," said William crushingly. Again he paused. "What sort of mint?"

"Bulth-eyeth."

"Oh," said William.

Violet Elizabeth evidently considered that the strategic moment had arrived for the final assault. She trotted quickly up to the group and held out a paper bag.

"Have one, William?"

"No, thanks," said William, but his tone lacked resolution.

"I've *thaid* I'm thorry," said Violet Elizabeth, employing the note of mournful reproach again.

"All right," said William ungraciously, taking a sweet from the bag. "Thanks."

She handed it to the others, and they each took a sweet, imitating the gruff ungraciousness of William's "Thanks."

"Where are you going, William?" said Violet Elizabeth.

William hesitated, realising a little regretfully that bull's-eyes must be paid for by whatever coin is demanded in return.

"We're goin' to the tadpole pond at the Manor," he said shortly.

"Can I come, too, William?" said Violet Elizabeth.

"No," said William, considering his account settled.

"Why not?"

" 'Cause we don't want you."

But they all knew that she would go with them. William was not a boy to treasure grievances, and the unwanted presence of Violet Elizabeth was such a normal part of his life's background that he would have had a vague sense of something missing had it not been there.

"I dunno whether we ought to keep goin' to the tadpole pond," said Douglas, who was occasionally troubled by scruples of conscience about their more lawless proceedings, though he never allowed such scruples to interfere with his actions.

"Well, ole Miss Maurice used to let us," said William.

"Yes, but she's gone now, and this new man's got the place. *He* never said we could."

"Well, we never asked him," said William, as if

this placed the whole situation upon a lawful footing.
"Anyway, he's not stopped us yet."

" 'Cause he's not found us," said Douglas.

"Well, he won't, either," said William, "if we go
on bein' careful. That hole in the hedge takes us jus'
to the tadpole pond, an' you can't see that from the
house."

"Pr'aps we'd *better* ask him," said Douglas, absently
kicking a stone across the road.

"I don't see it'd do any good," said William,
kicking the stone back. "We'd have to go on goin'
there whatever he said, 'cause it's the only decent
pond anywhere round."

They were in sight of the big iron gates leading to
the Manor now. Suddenly a car shot out and turned
in their direction.

At the wheel sat a tall thick-set man in chauffeur's
uniform with a face that would have been good-looking
had it not been for the ill-tempered curves of his lips
and the scowl that enveloped his rather close-set eyes.

Next him sat a small withered-looking man, with a
thin lined face and shifty short-sighted eyes, wearing
a loud check sports coat.

The car shot down the lane at a terrific speed,
scattering the Outlaws to right and left. Ginger,
William and Violet Elizabeth took refuge in the
ditch, and Henry and Douglas clung to the hedge
on the other side of the road.

The man in the sports coat leant from the window and
poured out a stream of curses at Henry and Douglas,
while the chauffeur shook his fist savagely at the other
three. The car passed on out of sight, and the five sat
by the roadside gazing after it.

"*Gosh!*" said William. "Fancy carryin' on like that

THE MAN IN THE SPORTS COAT LEANT FROM THE WINDOW
AND POURED OUT A STREAM OF CURSES AT HENRY
AND DOUGLAS.

when we weren't doin' anythin' but walkin' down the road!"

"An' kickin' stones," Douglas reminded him.

"Well, we weren't in his way. Gosh! He might have killed us."

"He wouldn't've cared if he had," said Douglas.

"He'd got an awful face," said Henry.

"An' his chauffeur's wasn't much better."

"Face like a monkey, he'd got."

"An' the chauffeur'd got a face like a toad."

"Gosh! The things he *said*."

"I bet there were some words that even Robert doesn't know," said William meditatively.

"He wathn't," said Violet Elizabeth, elevating her small nose as she contributed her quota to the discussion with an air of deep worldly wisdom, "he wathn't a gentleman."

"Well, anyway," said William, "we know he's out now. We can go to the tadpole pond all right."

They walked on down the lane to the big iron gates and stood gazing up the drive at the Manor House. It was a large, rather forbidding-looking house, four-square and fortress-like, with two rows of blank windows that seemed to peer suspiciously at the group of small boys who stood by the gate. There was even something vaguely threatening about it.

"I wish Miss Maurice hadn't gone," said Ginger. "It looked sort of diff'rent then. She had flowers an' things an' the windows open. . . ."

"P'raps he doesn't want flowers," said William. "I bet I wouldn't either. You're always gettin' into rows for knockin' vases of them over. I wouldn't have carpets, either, then you couldn't get into rows for spillin' things on them. P'raps he's got a bit of sense."

"I bet he hasn't," said Ginger. "Not with that face. Oh, come on."

"I say," said William, "we could go straight in by the gates if we wanted to, now we know he's out."

"We'd better not," said Douglas nervously. "There might be gardeners an' they can be jolly savage, can gardeners."

"I bet I could get away from any ole gard'ner, once I started runnin'," said William.

"You couldn't if he thet bloodhoundth on to you," said Violet Elizabeth.

"Oh, shut up," said William.

"Come on," said Douglas. "Let's go round to the hole in the hedge."

They walked about twenty yards down the road to a spot where a well-worn hole in the hedge marked the frequent passage of their small but solid persons.

"Here we are," said William. "I'll go first . . ."

They went through the hole in their usual order—first William, then Ginger, then Henry, then Douglas, then Violet Elizabeth scrambling frantically and wailing, "Wait for me, William."

It was just as Violet Elizabeth had finally emerged on the further side of the hole that they heard Hubert Lane's voice in the lane outside.

"Trespassing!" he said. "I'll tell on you."

William stood facing him across the hedge and wondering whether it was worth while getting back through the hole to deal with him in person. He decided that it wasn't.

"Oh, you will, will you?" he said.

"Yes, I will," said Hubert, gaining courage from the fact that the hedge was evidently to continue to serve as a bulwark. "I'll tell the police."

William gave a short laugh as he assumed one of his many imaginary characters.

"They'll be jolly amused if you do," he said.

"Why?" said Hubert, who was notoriously inquisitive.

"Gosh! Fancy you not knowin'," said William, with another short laugh.

"Knowin' what?" said Hubert.

"P'raps I'd better not tell you," said William.

"Tell me what?" said Hubert.

"About me and the p'lice," said William.

"What about you an' the police?" said Hubert.

"Well," William looked round as if for eavesdroppers, then lowered his voice. "Well, I don't want everyone to know, but we work together."

"Who work together?"

"Me an' the p'lice. I help 'em catch thieves an' things."

Hubert goggled and gaped. He was a credulous as well as an inquisitive boy.

"I don't believe you," he said.

"I jolly well don't want you to," said William. "Why——" He paused, awaiting inspiration. Inspiration came. "Only yesterday the p'lice were sayin' that the fewer people knew about it the better."

So convinced was William himself of the truth of the statement that it almost convinced Hubert.

He stared at William, open-mouthed.

"So you'd better be careful what you say about me to the p'lice," said William, "or you'll be gettin' into trouble yourself."

Then he turned on his heel and led the way down the shrubbery path that came out at the pond.

The spell of William's presence removed, Hubert's natural common sense reasserted itself.

"I don't believe you," he shouted.

William turned. "You wait!" he said. "You'll believe me all right before you've finished."

"Yah! I'll tell on you."

"All right, tell," said William, "an' see what happens to you."

An uncertain sound, compounded of fear, defiance, resentment and incredulity, was Hubert's only answer.

"Shall we go back an' chase him?" said Ginger.

"No," said William, "he's not worth it. 'Sides, we haven't got time. It'll be lunch-time before we know where we are."

They walked in single file along the path.

"Why did you tell him all that stuff, William?" said Douglas.

"Jus' sort of pulling his leg an'—an'—an' it *might* sort of be true."

"How?"

"You never know," said William vaguely. "Things *happen*, you know. It seems sort of poss'ble sometimes when you're thinking about it by yourself."

"*I* don't think it's poss'ble," said Douglas. "Not catchin' thieves."

"I onthe met a boy that'd caught a mouthe," said Violet Elizabeth.

"Oh, shut up," said William.

They had reached the pond now. It stood, large and dark and inviting, shadowed by trees.

"Come on!" shouted William exultantly, leaping down to the muddy edge.

For the next quarter of an hour they worked hard, transferring tadpoles from their native haunts to

William's jam jar. William's handkerchief did gallant service, assisting him in scooping tadpoles out of the mud and transferring them to the jam jar that was kept within the reach of all four. Violet Elizabeth contented herself with applauding their efforts and attending to the casualties.

"Hereth a little tadpole you've dropped, Ginger."

"Oo, William! You are *clever* to get all thothe at onthe. Be careful of the teeny one. . . ."

At last they stood, proudly surveying the result of their labour.

"I should think we've got about fifty," said Douglas. "It's jolly good."

"Did you know," said Henry impressively, "that all the world was tadpoles once? An' then they turned into animals. An' then they turned into men."

"Gosh! What a tale!" said William. "I don't believe a word of it."

"It's true," said Henry. "It was in a book."

"A book of fairy tales. I bet it said they turned into fairies."

"No, it didn't. It said they turned into animals. An' then into men."

"Well, it's not poss'ble. . . . I say!"

"Yes?"

William was surveying the dark surface of the pond. "I shouldn't be surprised if there's a monster there. A pre-historic sea-monster. They hide up in ponds an' they come out once every hundred years."

Violet Elizabeth drew away nervously.

"I don't like thea-monthterth," she said.

"I don't believe *that*," said Henry. "I'd rather b'lieve my tale than that."

"Hadn't we better be goin' home now?" said Douglas.

But they were loath to leave the fascinating spot.

"I bet it's not lunch-time yet," said William.

As he spoke, the church clock struck one.

"That's half-past twelve, or one o'clock," said Ginger.

"I bet it's half-past twelve," said William. "Let's see who can throw a stone furthest into it."

"Can I have a little tadpole of my own, pleathe, William?" said Violet Elizabeth.

"What d'you want it for?"

"I want to thee it turn into a fairy."

"It doesn't turn into a fairy, you little idiot," said William.

"It turns into an animal," said Henry.

"Well, I'd like to thee it turn into an animal," said Violet Elizabeth. "Can I choothe what animal it turnth into? I'd like a giraffe."

"It turns into a frog," said Douglas.

"I don't like frogth," said Violet Elizabeth.

"Come on!" said William. "Let's try throwin' stones."

"Can we play houtheth?" said Violet Elizabeth without much hope. "With you going to the offith an' me goin' thopping an' cooking the mealth."

"*No*," thundered William. "We're goin' to throw stones."

"All right," said Violet Elizabeth resignedly. "Thall we have thome more bulth-eyeth?"

They chose a shady spot on the bank of the pond and sat in a row, idly throwing stones into the water and sucking bull's-eyes.

"Mine went further than yours."

"It didn't."

"It did."

"I say, he mus' be jolly rich," said William suddenly. "Livin' in a place like this. There's miles an' *miles* of garden."

"An' a jolly dull sort of garden, too," said Ginger.

"Yes," agreed William. "Jus' like grown-ups, havin' miles an' miles of garden an' jus' dull things like flowers and grass in it. I bet *that* went further than yours."

"It didn't."

"It did."

"S'pose you had all this garden an' all the money in the world, what would you do with it?"

"I'd fill it with wild animals same as the Zoo," said Ginger. "It'd be jolly excitin'."

"I'd turn it all into a big pond an' have tadpoles an' ships in it," said Henry.

"I'd have trains goin' in it with stations an' things," said Douglas. "*Real* ones."

"What would you have, William?"

William considered. "I'd have a big fair with swings an' roundabouts an' hoop-la's an' Wild Sea Waves an' Walls of Death an' ice-cream stalls an' *everything*. An' I'd have it goin' on all day long every day always. An' I'd go out to it soon as I'd finished breakfast an' stay there till it was bedtime an'——" He froze into sudden immobility in the act of throwing a stone. "Gosh!" he whispered. "He's comin' back. He must've jus' been to the village."

Through the trees they could see the car turning in at the gates. It stopped just inside the gateway.

"Why's it stopped?" said Ginger. "Can you see?"

"No."

It had stopped because Hubert Lane had stopped it. Smarting under the indignity of his capture earlier in the morning, annoyed that he had been even for a moment taken in by William's fantastic claims, he had decided to avenge himself on his foes by informing the new tenant of the Manor that they were trespassing on his property. He had hung about near the gate till he was rewarded, rather to his surprise, by the speedy return of the car. He held out his hand. The car braked to a stop. The man in the check sports coat put his face out of the window, with an expression that was enquiring though not encouraging. Hubert felt a strong inclination to turn and flee, but he conquered it.

"There's four boys trespassing in your garden down by your pond," he said.

"All right," said the man shortly, "and clear off yourself."

Hubert, needing no second bidding, cleared off. The car drove on up the drive to the front door.

The chauffeur opened the car door and got out. But he did not open the car door for the man in the check sports coat. He stood in the drive and lit a cigarette, waiting till the man joined him. Then he jerked his head in the direction of the pond.

"Clear those kids out and be quick about it," he said, adding, "and see they don't come back."

"I'll tan their hides," said the man.

"No, we don't want any scenes," said the chauffeur. "Just clear them out."

"O.K., boss," said the man, starting off in the direction of the pond.

But he had no need to take any active part in the clearance. The Outlaws and Violet Elizabeth had seen him coming and were half-way through the shrubbery on their way to the hole in the hedge.

"Gosh!" panted William when they had reached the safety of the road. "That was a narrow escape, all right. I bet ole Monkey Face'd've killed us if he'd caught us."

"Yah!" jeered Hubert Lane, coming out of his hiding place behind a tree. "Thought you worked with the police! Yah!"

"You wait," said William. "You just——"

But Hubert Lane wasn't waiting. He had already started for home as fast as his rather fat legs could carry him.

"Oh, come on," said William. "He's not worth runnin' after. I bet it's lunch-time. . . . Now remember what we've fixed to do this afternoon."

Chapter 6

William put his jar of tadpoles under the hat-stand and glanced at the hall clock.

His hit-or-miss guess at the time had happened to be right, and the stroke of the church clock had signified half-past twelve and not one o'clock. He was only a few minutes late.

Emily was coming down the hall from the kitchen with a dish of potatoes in her hand.

"I seed you condescended to bring back the bread-knife," she said.

"When I borrow things," said William with dignity, "I bring them back."

"Oh, you do, do you?" said Emily with a wealth of sarcasm in her voice. She paused and looked at him. "An' what are you to-day," she said, "if one may make so bold as to ask?"

"I shan't tell you," said William. "I'm something jolly important."

Between Emily and William was the bond of long years of alternating enmity and amity. Beneath their sparring they were deeply attached to each other.

"Well, as long as you don't need the whole dinner service *an'* the carvin'-knife for it——" said Emily.

"Huh!" said William. "I'll want somethin' more deadly than a carvin'-knife when I get goin'."

" 'Ow many winders 'ave you broke so far?" said Emily. "I may chance to see Mr. Heppleback this afternoon, so I might as well warn 'im."

"Windows?" said William, as if the question was unintelligible to him. "I dunno what you mean."

"They're glass things what you look through," explained Emily.

"I bet you'd break 'em with jus' lookin' through 'em, then," said William. "I bet if I was a window and saw your face I'd——"

"Emily!" called Mrs. Brown from the dining-room.

Emily heaved a deep sigh, resumed her expression of patient suffering and proceeded on her way to the dining-room.

William stayed to brush his hair back with his hand and to put his cap at a rakish angle on to the deer's head, pulling it well down over one eye and leaving the other clear, then entered the dining-room and took his seat at the table.

"Sorry I'm a bit late," he said, emphasising the 'bit' and glancing at the clock whose fingers stood at eight minutes past one.

"Don't apologise," said Mr. Brown. "The shock of seeing you on time for anything would probably prostrate us for weeks."

Mr. Brown was in a good temper. Having missed the late train, and remembering that it was Saturday anyway, he had decided to take the morning off and had spent it with Robert on the golf links.

"Huh?" said William uncomprehendingly.

"Your father means," translated Mrs. Brown, "that you must try to be more punctual in future."

"Oh, that!" said William, losing interest. "I thought he was sayin' somethin' diff'rent."

"Did you wash your hands?" said Mrs. Brown.

"Yes," said William, hastily removing them from sight.

"What with?" said Ethel, who had caught a glimpse of them. "Soot?"

"Let me see them, William," said Mrs. Brown.

William made a grimace at Ethel and presented for his mother's inspection the backs of a pair of tightly-clenched fists.

"I want to see the insides, William," said Mrs. Brown with quiet ruthlessness.

Reluctantly he opened his hands, trying ineffectually to hide the worst parts with his fingers.

"*William!*" said Mrs. Brown in horror.

"I've sort of got a darker skin than most people," explained William.

"And a thicker," said Robert.

"Go and wash your hands again, William," said Mrs. Brown.

William went upstairs to the bathroom, washed his hands, made a whirlpool of the water in the hand-basin, into which he put a dainty pink nail-brush of Ethel's, imagining it to be a small imperilled craft, watched the whirlpool die down, made it again, watched it die down, made it again, dried his hands on the towel, inspected the newly-mended geyser with interest, went downstairs, changed the angle of his cap on the deer's head by putting it as far back as he could, imparting a look of foolish simplicity to the long-suffering face, then re-entered the dining-room.

Emily was hovering round the table with the vegetable dishes. It was no part of Emily's many duties to wait at table, but she generally hovered round, because she liked to know what the family was talking about.

"Did you touch that geyser again, William?" said Mr. Brown.

"No," said William.

"A few more depredations on that scale," said Mr. Brown, "and we shall be joining the ranks of the homeless."

"What homeless?" said William, taking his seat.

"It may interest you to know," said Mr. Brown, "that there are thousands of homeless people in this country, so you might try to spare what few household effects still remain to us."

"Your father means that you must try to be less destructive, dear," said Mrs. Brown. "Now let me see your hands." William let her see them. "They don't look much better."

"I've given them a good wash."

"Did you empty the hand-basin?"

William wrinkled his brow, trying to remember what he'd done with his whirlpool.

"I think I did," he said uncertainly.

"I expect the towel has to be seen to be believed," said Ethel.

"I wish you'd leave me alone," growled William. He took the plate that his mother was passing him. "Shepherd's pie. Good! I say, why do they call it shepherd's pie?"

"Get on with your lunch and don't talk so much."

Emily handed him the potatoes, and, leaning as far back in his chair as he could, he furtively put out a hand to untie the strings that secured her overall. Emily had expected the manoeuvre (it was an old one) and neatly circumvented it.

"William!" said Mrs. Brown, who had seen him.

"It's all right, mum," said Emily, and, going to the

door, added darkly, "I got worse things than that to put up with in this house."

"Oh, dear!" sighed Mrs. Brown as the door closed on her.

For the next few minutes William gave his whole attention to the consumption of his shepherd's pie, receiving stoically such comments on his table manners as his elders chose to throw at him in the intervals of their discussion of gold, shopping, neighbours, and the inadequacy of bus and train service. The keen edge of his hunger blunted, he turned his attention to their conversation.

"I think we shall have to go," his mother was saying.

"Go where?" said William.

"Be quiet, William. No one was speaking to you."

"All right," said William. "I only said, 'Go where?'"

"*All* of us?" groaned Mr. Brown. "And on *Sunday?*"

"And to the *Lanes!*" groaned Ethel.

"Well, dear, it's a party she's getting up specially to meet this film star."

"What film star?" said William.

"Be quiet, William."

"All right," said William. "I only said, 'What film star?'"

"The effect on the nerves of the continual sound of your voice, William," said Mr. Brown, "is something that beggars description."

"Your father means you mustn't talk so much," translated Mrs. Brown.

"Oh," said William.

"She's taken Honeysuckle Cottage for the summer, you know," said Ethel.

"Who has?" said Mr. Brown. "I don't think much of these potatoes. Where did you get them?"

"This Gloria Gaye," said Mrs. Brown. "I got them from the greengrocer's as usual."

"What Gloria Gaye?" said Mr. Brown. "There's no taste in them at all."

"She's a film star," said Mrs. Brown. "Perhaps it's the weather. It does affect them."

"Never heard of her," said Mr. Brown testily, "and I think you ought to speak very strongly to him about it. Might as well be eating mangel-worzels."

"I've eaten mangel-worzels," said William. "They aren't bad."

"Be quiet, William."

"All right," said William. "I only said I'd——" He met his father's eye, and lapsed into silence.

"Once let these tradespeople think they can give you any rubbish they like, and you might as well take poison and be done with it," said Mr. Brown.

William opened his mouth to speak, met his father's eye, and closed it again, transferring his attention to the roly-poly pudding that Emily was just bringing in.

"Can I have an end, please?" he said.

"You'll have what you're given," said Mrs. Brown.

"Thanks," said William, knowing that he'd get an end. "I like 'em 'cause they're crinkly."

"Have you heard of her, Robert?" said Mrs. Brown.

"Who?" said Robert.

"Whom," said Ethel with an air of triumph.

"Too pedantic. . . . Who," said Robert.

"Whom," persisted Ethel.

"Gloria Gaye," said Mrs. Brown.

"Yes," said Robert. "Yes . . . she was in 'Love in a Mist'."

There was a fatuous far-away expression on his face. William knew that expression. He transferred his attention from the roly-poly to Robert.

"Well, if you think," said Mr. Brown, "that I'm going to waste a Sunday afternoon in this way . . ."

"I think we ought to, dear," said Mrs. Brown again placidly.

"I do, too," said Robert. "I mean—she's a stranger in the neighbourhood. She probably feels a little lonely, and—well, one does owe a sort of duty to one's neighbours."

"I didn't notice the same interest in the new tenant at the Manor," said Ethel dryly.

"That's different," said Robert. "He's a flash town type. He can look after himself."

"And I suppose Gloria Gaye can't?"

"Well, she's only a girl," said Robert. "She doesn't look more than about nineteen in her pictures."

"She's thirty, if she's a day," said Ethel.

"She isn't!"

"She is!"

"She isn't!"

"Children!" said Mrs. Brown.

"What I mean is——" said Robert.

"What you mean is," said Ethel, "that she's the most wonderful girl you've ever seen in your life, and——"

"Oh shut up," said Robert.

William had been listening intently to the conversation. His eyes had gone from Robert to Ethel, from Ethel to Robert. . . . They remained fixed on Robert, and a slow smile spread over his face.

Ethel, whom few things escaped, noticed his smile.

"And what are *you* smiling at?" she said.

"Me?" said William, hastily summoning his blankest look. "Me? Was I smiling? I don't know . . . Sometimes I jus' smile for hours an' I don't know what I'm smilin' at. I once heard of a man——"

"That'll do," said Mr. Brown shortly. "We don't want a lecture on it. Get on with your lunch."

William attacked his second helping of roly-poly with silent gusto, but with a preoccupied mind. Occasionally he raised his eyes to glance speculatively at Robert. His plans for the afternoon were forming themselves—plans that were eventually to secure him a bicycle . . . but in the meantime a bicycle would be helpful in the carrying out of them.

"Are you using your bicycle this afternoon, Robert?" he said casually.

"Yes, I am," said Robert, "and, if I wasn't, I wouldn't let you and those Dead End Kids get their hands on it."

"I thought p'raps there was some—some little errand you'd like me to do for you on it," said William.

"Well, there isn't," said Robert shortly.

"It was a very kind thought of William's, Robert dear," said Mrs. Brown reproachfully.

No amount of bitter experience ever damped Mrs. Brown's belief in the innate nobility of her younger son.

Robert gave a sardonic snort.

"P'raps you'd like me to clean it for you?" said William.

"And p'raps I wouldn't," said Robert.

"It's very thoughtful of you, William dear," said Mrs. Brown. "Robert's grateful to you."

"He isn't," said William without rancour.

"You're right there," said Robert. "I'm not. When I remember the last time you cleaned it——"

"Oh, that!" said William hastily. "Yes, I was sorry about that. You see, when I borrowed those nuts from it to mend my launch, I didn't know it'd make all that diff'rence to the bike. I didn't know they were as necess'ry as all that. Anyway, that was over a week ago. I'm a good bit older now."

"Well, you can stop wasting your breath trying to pinch my bicycle for this afternoon."

"All right," said William, not at all offended. He hadn't really expected Robert to be taken in by the ruse. "Can I have another helping of pudding?"

"No, dear," said Mrs. Brown. "You've had three."

"Can I go, please?"

"Yes. Fold up your table napkin. *Fold* it, dear. Don't *maul* it. All right. You can go."

William rose and went slowly and thoughtfully from the room.

"Can't we *do* anything about William?" groaned Ethel. "Can't we send him to an orphanage or something?"

"No, dear," said Mrs. Brown placidly. "You see, he isn't an orphan."

"He soon will be at this rate," said Mr. Brown. "A geyser and two windows in one week!"

"And the *filthy* state he goes about in!" said Ethel.

"He means well," said Mrs. Brown, "and, when he's got his best suit on and just had his hair cut, I sometimes think he looks quite sweet."

They laughed.

"Well, I do," said Mrs. Brown, joining in the laugh.

Mr. Brown rose.

"Going to give me a return, Robert?" he said.

"Sorry, I can't," said Robert. "I've got to go through those darned cricket club accounts this afternoon. . . ."

* * *

William wandered slowly round the house, his hands in his pockets, his mind absorbed by thought. He had fixed on Gloria Gaye as Robert's future wife. Robert's interest in her had obviously been aroused. The trouble was that Robert's interest was so easily aroused. . . . The pathway of Robert's life was strewn with such interests. The girls who had been the most wonderful girls whom Robert had ever seen, but who a few weeks later had evidently failed to live up to the first promise of the acquaintanceship, were as numerous as the flowers in spring-time. And Robert never seemed seriously to contemplate marriage. Robert, William decided, must be made to contemplate marriage, and the idea of marriage must be firmly harnessed to his new interest in Gloria Gaye.

Passing the drawing-room window, he peeped in cautiously. Robert was seated at the bureau, busy with the cricket club accounts. William entered by the french window and seated himself in an arm-chair by the fireplace. There was a long silence. Robert did not turn round from the bureau, but his whole person expressed annoyance at the interruption. Moreover, not being very good at arithmetic, he was counting on his fingers, and he had an uncomfortable suspicion that William would see that he was doing it, though he kept his fingers well out of William's sight. Actually, William was too much occupied by his thoughts to notice, and, even if he had noticed, would have seen nothing strange in it, as that was the way he always did his own sums.

He was wondering how best to begin the confidential conversation he meant to have with Robert.

Robert broke the silence.

"What are you doing here?" he said curtly without turning round.

"Jus' sittin' qui'tly," said William.

"Well, if you're going to stay here, you can go on sitting quietly," said Robert.

"All right," agreed William, returning to his mental speculation. But, though he did not speak again, he was not a boy who could ever sit in perfect silence. His best friends could not claim for him the qualities of tranquillity or repose. Sunk deep in thought, he coughed and fidgeted. Absently he banged a brass ash-tray on to a table with his hand and rattled the fire-irons with his foot.

At last Robert wheeled round with a frown of exasperation.

"Haven't you anything to do?" he said.

"No," replied William.

"Can't you go and play with your friends?"

"No," said William. "They're busy."

His friends were, he hoped, engaged in the same activities as he was engaged in.

Robert groaned and returned to his accounts.

And then William, having rallied his forces and planned his campaign, opened the attack.

"How old are you, Robert?" he said.

"Sixteen and six," said Robert. "Twenty-one and shut up."

"Twenty-one!" echoed William incredulously and emitted a long whistle of surprise.

"Well, why shouldn't I be twenty-one?" said Robert. "One pound four and ninepence. . . ."

William gave a short laugh.

"Well, I mus' say I didn't think you were *quite* as old as that. Twenty-one's jolly old not to be married. Seems to me most people are married by the time they've got to that age. Twenty-one! Gosh!"

"Go away!" said Robert, running his hand through his hair. "Annual dinner and dance . . ."

"Seems to me," said William, "that if anyone's goin' to get married they ought to've thought about it by the time they get to twenty-one. *Gosh! Twenty-one!*"

There was no doubt that as an actor William belonged to the ham school and overdid his effects.

"Will you shut up!" said Robert savagely.

"I mean," said William, clinging doggedly to his theme, "you don't want to wait till you're *old* to get married. I mean, old people look jolly silly gettin' married. You remember when ole Mr. Doune got married, how——"

Robert rose abruptly, collected his papers and went from the room, slamming the door.

William sighed. The whole business was turning out more difficult than he had thought it was going to be, but he did not intend to abandon it on that account.

Robert had spread out his papers on the dining-room table. He did not look up when William appeared in the doorway, leaning carelessly against the doorpost.

"It's *you* I'm thinkin' of, Robert," he said.

Robert ignored him.

"I MEAN," SAID WILLIAM, CLINGING DOGGEDLY TO
HIS THEME, "YOU DON'T WANT TO WAIT TILL YOU'RE
TOO *OLD* TO GET MARRIED"

"Gloria Gaye's a beautiful girl," continued William.

Robert added up a column of figures and made it come to £10 6s. 0d.

"I've seen her in films and she's jolly good, isn't she?" William went on.

Robert added up the same column of figures and made it come to £4 5s. 3½d.

William advanced into the room and took the seat at the table next Robert's.

"If I was twenty-one, Robert," he said earnestly, "I'd want to marry her before I got so old she wouldn't have me."

There was a short silence.

"They like flowers . . ." said William.

Robert stood up and addressed him slowly and impressively.

"William," he said, "if you don't leave me alone, I'll wring your dirty little neck."

William rubbed his neck, then examined his fingers. "It's not really dirty," he said. "This dirt was on my fingers to start with. I washed it this mornin', anyway, and nothin's touched it since but air. I can't help air bein' dirty, can I?"

"I'm going to sit in the garden," Robert continued, ignoring this dissertation, "and if you come within ten yards of me—so help me—I'll crown you."

He went out into the garden, took a deck-chair from the veranda, set it up at the end of the lawn, and continued his interrupted work.

"Twenty-seven and sixpence, twenty-eight and sixpence . . . one pound nine and sixpence. . . ."

The hall window was opened and William's face appeared.

"Fancy!" said William. "Twenty-one an' not married!"

Robert wheeled round in the chair, closed his account book and flung it at William's head.

There was a sound of splintering glass as it went through the hall window.

Chapter 7

William had beat a hasty retreat after the episode of the hall window, and now he was returning slowly, warily, ready to beat another and yet more hasty retreat should Robert be lying in wait for him.

But Robert had disappeared. Only the deck-chair and the broken hall window remained to mark the scene.

Dismissing the incident from his mind, William set to work on the second part of his programme. He had, he hoped, planted a seed in Robert's mind that would eventually flower and bear fruit. After their long and confidential conversation, Robert's thoughts must surely be turning to marriage . . . and Gloria Gaye was the obvious goal to which those thoughts must tend. But Gloria Gaye herself must be prepared. Robert, a quick worker on some occasions, was a slow worker on others. William suspected that Gloria Gaye's glamour and fame would paralyse even the redoubtable Robert. He had more than once seen Robert, in the presence of some local beauty, tongue-tied, embarrassed, hotly self-conscious, making no headway at all. That must not happen in Gloria Gaye's case. Robert must be firmly established in Gloria's eyes as her suitor, so that, before they met, the foundations of the whole affair should be well and truly laid. The idea of getting

Robert married was taking firm hold of William's mind. Not only would it assure him a bicycle, but the thought of a Robertless home was, on the whole, a pleasant one. Robert, of course, was no worse than any other elder brother, but it was in the nature of elder brotherhood to snub, repress and employ disciplinary measures that seemed to the victim little short of brutal. Therefore, Robert must be married. And, as Robert took to looks and glamour as a duck takes to water, Gloria Gaye would surely finish off the business more effectively and speedily than anyone else.

He drew a sigh of relief when he saw that the garden was empty . . . then, cautiously, glancing at all the windows of the house to make sure that no one was watching him, he sidled up to the rose bed.

"You leave them roses alone!" said a gruff voice.

William had forgotten that it was one of the two days a week on which Hobbins, a jobbing gardener, came to the Browns' house and tended such portions of the garden as William's activities left capable of being tended. Between William and Hobbins—a small but ferocious man, who wore a large cloth cap and much darned pullover even through the hottest days of summer—reigned a deep and bitter enmity, unassuaged by any of the affection that existed between William and Emily.

"I said, leave 'em alone," he growled.

"All right," said William. "I was only lookin' at 'em. That's what they're there for—isn't it?—to be *looked* at. I thought that was what people put flowers in gardens for—for people to *look* at 'em." He gave his short sarcastic laugh. "It's news to *me* you can't look at flowers."

Hobbins, who was a man of few words, growled

again and returned to his weeding of the herbaceous border. William strolled about the garden in an innocent abstracted fashion as if enjoying the fresh air and the beauty of his surroundings . . . waiting till Hobbins should become so deeply absorbed in his task that he would have no further attention to spare for him. But whatever Hobbins was doing, one steely suspicious eye seemed to remain fixed on William. There was a moment when he had his back so squarely turned that William thought he might safely make another attempt, but, before he had even put out his hand to the nearest rose, "You leave them roses alone," came from behind the squarely turned back.

"All right," said William dispiritedly. "I was only goin' to see what they *feel* like. There's no lor against that, is there? I only thought it'd be *int'restin'* to see what they feel like."

Hobbins offered no comment on this. William hadn't expected him to. An idea of making a quick raid and then taking to his heels was dismissed as soon as it was conceived. Despite his smallness Hobbins was nimble-footed and had no compunction in laying complaints before Mr. Brown on what William considered to be wholly inadequate grounds.

William wandered over to the herbaceous border and watched Hobbins at work for some time. Then he cleared his throat and said in a pleasant but rather unnatural voice (for William never found it easy to assume an alien character), "Can I help you at all Hobbins?"

"You can stand out of my light," growled Hobbins.

William stood out of his light and considered his next move.

"You know," he said at last, "I've been thinkin

I'd like to be a gard'ner when I grow up, an' I'd like a bit of practice. I think it'd be *good* for me to have a bit of practice in gard'nin', so's to be ready to be a gard'ner when I grow up."

He paused but received no encouragement. He hadn't expected any.

"You see," he went on, "if I could do a bit of gard'nin' now, it'd sort of help me later on when I'm a gard'ner."

There was a silence during which Hobbins pulled up a dandelion, a few strands of toad flax, a clump of sorrel and a sycamore seedling.

William perceived that it was no good beating about the bush any longer and that he might as well come to the point.

"Can I—can I cut off the dead blooms?" he said. "Jus' for practice in bein' a gard'ner?"

"Naw," said Hobbins shortly.

William sighed. The plan had been a subtle one—he had thought that, in cutting off the dead blooms, he could surely secrete among them enough live ones to make up the bouquet that he had decided to present to Gloria Gaye on Robert's behalf—but evidently it wasn't going to work.

Then he saw his mother, setting off from the side door with a shopping basket, and had a fresh inspiration. It sometimes worked to go to one authority over the head of another. He hadn't much hope, but it was worth trying.

"Mother," he said, approaching her, "may I cut off the dead blooms in the garden for you?"

"Ask Hobbins, dear," said Mrs. Brown absently and went on her way to the gate.

William returned dejectedly to Hobbins, standing

near him for a few moments, sunk in thought. Then he glanced round the garden, and his face brightened.

Hobbins had spent the morning clearing out the "seeded" forget-me-nots from the borders, and they lay in heaps on the rubbish pile. Though "seeded", a few blooms clung to them, here and there, and the foliage, though brown in parts, held a trace of green. They could still—at a pinch—be called flowers, and they were better than nothing.

"Can I have those?" he said, pointing to them.

Hobbins stood up, straightening his back slowly and scowling from William to the forget-me-nots, from the forget-me-nots to William.

"What d'you want 'em for?" he said suspiciously.

William conquered an inclination to say, "Mind your own business," and said with an attempt at dignity, "I want to take 'em to a friend."

"Why?" said Hobbins.

"Why not?" said William. "People *do* take flowers to friends, don't they? They take flowers to them when they're ill, don't they? I've often heard of people takin' flowers to people when they're ill. I bet, if I'd ever been ill, people'd've brought me flowers."

"What's the matter with yer friend?" demanded Hobbins.

He had an idea that some deep plot against him was being hatched by the little devil, and he meant to get to the bottom of it.

"I don't know yet," hedged William. "Doctors can't tell straight off what's wrong with people, can they? It might be measles or—or—or"—he remembered an address given recently by a missionary at the school he attended—"or leprosy or anything." Measles sounded a bit tame, so he decided on leprosy. "It's prob'ly leprosy.

Well, if you grudge a few rotten ole flowers to a poor person what's ill with leprosy . . ."

But Hobbins had discovered an ants' nest near the root of his favourite peony and lost interest in William's involved recital.

Perceiving that his attention had wandered, William made his way to the rubbish heap and inspected his proposed offering. Seen at close quarters, it looked less inviting than it had looked from the distance, but still it belonged indisputably to a floral species and could be recognised as such even at the advanced stage at which it had arrived. Besides—William brightened still further when this thought occurred to him—the name, forget-me-not, conveyed a message that was suitable to the occasion. Yes, he must make the most of that. He picked up a handful of the wilting blooms and held them at arm's length to study the effect. Only a few blue petals adhered to them. He added another handful and decided that the effect was better. In fact, the more forget-me-nots there were, the more blue patches there were. Having realised this simple fact, he acted on it. He filled his arms with them. He took enough to load a wheel-barrow. Then, slowly, self-consciously, keeping his eyes fixed in front of him, he walked across the lawn before Hobbins' astonished gaze.

* * *

Gloria Gaye lay outstretched on her massage table. She was a glamorous blonde, and, if not quite in her first youth, not far out of it. A masseur, in a white coat, with an expression of intense boredom on his face (he had seen too many film stars, too often, and at too close quarters, to retain any illusions about them) was engaged in pummelling her, and a secretary

was sitting on a chair by the massage table, sorting out
the afternoon's post. The secretary was dark, pretty
and vivacious-looking. She wore a pair of horn-rimmed
spectacles, which occasionally she took off and twirled
round by the ear-piece, giving an impression of such
light-heartedness that one almost expected the raucous
grating of a joy-rattle to issue from them.

"*Not* the fan-mail, for heaven's sake, Kay," groaned
Miss Gaye. "I've come here for a rest cure. Answer
them, forge my signature, send my photograph, but,
for heaven's sake, don't read them to me. Anything
else?"

"A few bills . . ." said Miss Petworth.

"Burn them. Anything else?"

"Press cutting."

"Keep anything sensible and burn the rest."

"By sensible, I presume," said Miss Petworth,
twirling the spectacles, "you mean such as recognise
your genius, your beauty, your Cleopatra-like charm?"

Miss Gaye laughed—her well-known musical ripple,
which the masseur rather maliciously cut up into a series
of short sharp barks.

"How well you know me, darling!" she said.

"I ought to by this time," said Miss Petworth.

"Anything else?"

"Someone says they've seen 'Love in a Mist'
fifteen times, and cried each time."

"Tell them to see a doctor. Anything else?"

"Someone wants to know if you love dear little
children?"

"Tell them I don't. Anything else?"

"Someone——"

A series of thundering knocks resounded through
the cottage, seeming to shake it to its foundations.

"Heavens alive!" said Miss Gaye. "What's that?"

"Sounded like the police," said the masseur hopefully.

"Or a fire-engine," said Miss Petworth.

"Look out of the window, darling," said Miss Gaye, "and see what it is."

Miss Petworth went to the window and looked out, but the projecting porch hid the visitor from her.

"What is it?" said Miss Gaye.

"I can't see."

At that moment a second series of thundering knocks resounded through the cottage.

"My God! I can't stand this," said Miss Gaye. "I came here for a rest cure. Why doesn't that woman—whoever she is—go to the door?"

"She's out," Miss Petworth reminded her. "It's her afternoon. I'll go."

"Go quickly before it happens again," said Miss Gaye. "If it happens again, I shall go mad. I keep telling you I came here for a rest cure."

Miss Petworth twirled her spectacles, went down the steep narrow stairs and opened the front door. At first, there seemed to be nothing there but an enormous sheaf of drooping seeded forget-me-nots. Then she saw a pair of legs beneath them, and, peering through the cascades of wilting bloom, a stern anxious face. Behind this apparition was a small dog of indeterminate breed, wagging its tail in a tentative fashion as if unsure of its welcome.

Without waiting for an invitation, the apparition entered and dumped the burden on the small oak chest just inside the door. A cloud of forget-me-not seeds rose into the air, then settled on carpet, chest and the neighbouring furniture. Miss Petworth gazed in startled bewilderment at the small boy now revealed to her gaze.

William had looked fairly tidy when he set out from home, but, on reaching the gate of the cottage, it had occurred to him that he must do what he could to embellish his appearance for such an important occasion. He had laid his forget-me-nots on the ground and examined what he could see of his person. His suit looked fairly tidy, but his shoes were covered with mud from his visit to the Manor pond in the morning. He took off his cap and carefully removed the mud, replacing the now mud-encrusted cap at a careless angle on his unruly hair.

Then he considered his face. . . . He could not see his face, of course, but it was generally the target of unfavourable comments from his family, and he took for granted that it stood in its usual need of what attention he could give it. Absently, his mind wholly occupied by the momentous interview ahead of him, he drew out his handkerchief and rubbed it hard over cheek, nose, chin and forehead, forgetting the uses to which he had recently put that long-suffering article, and leaving a train of mingled mud and red paint over all his features.

Then, convinced that he had done all that was humanly possible to make himself presentable, he picked up the forget-me-nots and entered the gate.

"Yes?" said Miss Petworth faintly.

William noticed the forget-me-not seeds adhering to his coat and carefully brushed them off on to the floor. Then he looked at Miss Petworth with an air of stern and scowling resolution.

"I've brought these flowers for Miss Gloria Gaye," he said, "an' I want to speak to her."

"Won't you come in and sit down?" said Miss Petworth, motioning him into the little sitting-room.

"All right," said William, following her into the room and sitting down on a small settee.

"Miss Gaye's a very busy person, you know," said Miss Petworth.

"I'm busy, too," said William.

"And she's come here because she wants to rest," said Miss Petworth.

William considered this.

"Well, she can rest," he said. "She can go on restin' while I'm talking to her."

"You don't look a very restful person," said Miss Petworth.

"Well, it's not me that wants to rest, is it?" said William reasonably. "It's her. Tell her I won't stop her restin'."

"What do you want to speak to her about?" said Miss Petworth.

"About her gettin' married."

"About what?"

"About her gettin' married," said William, raising his voice and speaking rather irritably. He disliked having to repeat himself.

"But how? Why? I mean——"

"Look here," said William patiently. "It's no use me wastin' my time sayin' it all to you, when it's her I've come to say it to, is it?"

Miss Petworth blinked and gulped and turned to the door.

"I'll tell her you're here," she said as she went from the room.

She entered Miss Gaye's bedroom, twirling her spectacles.

"It's a young man, dear," she said. "He wants to see you."

Miss Gaye sat up.

"Who is it?"

"I don't know. He didn't give his name."

A certain interest invaded Miss Gaye's languor.

"Don't say that young Alistair has pursued me down here?"

"No, it isn't young Alistair."

"Which of them is it?"

"I've never seen him before."

"A new one?"

"A new one."

"Local?"

"Local. Or so I gather."

Miss Gaye gave rather a stagy groan.

"Don't they *know* that I'm down here for a rest?"

"I told him."

"What's he like? Good-looking?"

"Not good-looking, exactly, but there's plenty of character in his face. And he's very determined."

Miss Gaye gave a little giggle. "Sounds rather my type," she said.

"Shall we continue?" said the masseur, wearily cynical.

"In a minute," said Miss Gaye tartly. "You've broken my back and pounded my stomach to a jelly. Give me a second or two to get over it. I know that my back and stomach mean nothing to you, but . . ."

"On the contrary," said the masseur in a tone of exquisite politeness, "they have great weight with me."

"What exactly d'you mean by that?" said Miss Gaye, then to her secretary: "What does this young man want?"

"I gather that he wants to marry you."

"My God!" said Gloria Gaye. "Another of them?"

"Another of them," said Miss Petworth.

Miss Gaye drew her wrapper about her and cast a complacent glance at the reflection of her alluring face in the dressing-table mirror.

"I think you must see him, dear," said Miss Petworth. "He obviously isn't going away till you have done."

"Oh, very well," said Miss Gaye with an unconvincing show of reluctance.

The rest cure was proving unexpectedly boring, and almost any diversion would have been welcome. The diversion of a love-lorn youth was one that Miss Gloria Gaye had never failed to welcome in any circumstances. She turned to the masseur.

"I think we've had enough for to-day," she said distantly.

"As you please," said the masseur, beginning to pack up his implements.

He was a man who could endow the most ordinary expressions with a suggestion of subtle sarcasm.

"I don't like him," said Miss Gaye as the door closed behind him, "but he's the only man in London I can trust with my figure. . . . Now, darling, I'll wear the new blue and white, and get out those nylons that came yesterday."

Twenty minutes later, Miss Gaye descended the stairs, looking almost as bewitching as she had looked in "Love in a Mist". She opened the sitting-room door and stood for a second in the doorway in her favourite pose. But only for a second. . . . In the interval of waiting, it had occurred to William that he ought to present the bouquet in person to

Miss Gaye, and he had retrieved it from the hall chest.

As Miss Gaye entered the room, the armful was thrust at her unceremoniously, and she blinked and coughed and sneezed as the clouds of seeds settled in eyes, nose and throat. Weakly she let the whole thing fall on to the ground. . . . With a certain reproach in his manner, William collected it and dumped it on the settee.

"These forget-me-nots," he said, "are from someone what loves you with a most devouring passion."

Jumble, who was sitting by the settee, thumped his tail on the ground in applause. Miss Gaye looked from William to Jumble . . . and from Jumble back to William.

"I'll kill Kay for this," she said slowly.

But William had learnt his piece by heart and wasn't going to be side-tracked till he'd finished it.

"It's someone who think's you're the apple of his life an' wants to marry you." Then he suddenly remembered what Miss Petworth had said and added kindly: "Go on restin'. I don't want to stop you restin'."

Miss Gaye sat down, and the corner of her mouth began to twitch. She was not without a sense of humour, and she could take a joke against herself as well as anyone.

"What's your name?" she said.

"William."

"Well, William, I think it's very sweet of you, but don't you think I'm rather old to marry you?"

"*Me?*" said William recoiling in horror. "*Gosh!* I don't want to marry you."

"I thought that was the idea," said Miss Gaye mildly.

AS MISS GLORIA GAYE ENTERED THE ROOM THE ARMFUL
WAS THRUST AT HER UNCEREMONIOUSLY.

"No, I'm never goin' to marry," said William. "I don't like women—'cept my mother. No, it's Robert."

"Robert?"

"Yes, it's Robert that wants to marry you."

"Who's Robert?"

"He's my brother. He was too shy to come himself, so I've come for him."

Miss Gaye considered his explanation. "Shy? He's your—younger brother, perhaps?"

"*Young?*" said Wiliam. "No, he's old. Well, middle-aged. He's twenty-one."

"Oh."

"He loves you better than any of those men that love you on the pictures," went on William, warming to his theme, "but he wants a bit of help from you. I mean, he's shy. I mean, when you meet him, don't say anythin' about what I've told you an' don't mind if he seems diff'rent to what I've said about him, 'cause he loves you, all right, an' he wants to marry you. Nex' week, if you can fix it up." He took up his cap. "Well, I've finished now. I've not stopped you restin', have I? If you were goin' to marry that man that came downstairs, I wouldn't, if I was you. Robert's a bit mean an' bad-tempered, but I bet he's a jolly sight better than him. Well, I'll be goin' now." He looked down at Jumble with a softening of his grimly earnest expression. "That's my dog. He's a jolly fine dog, isn't he? He can beg and jump through a hoop. At least, he jumps through the hoop, if it's the only way he can get out. . . . Well, good-bye." He went to the door, then looked back at the settee. "You'd better put those flowers in water. They've been," with a sudden burst of honesty, "lyin' about a bit, but they're not so dead

as what they look. I bet they'll come round all right if
you put them in water. Well, good-bye."

He went out of the door, then put his head
back into the room. "You know what they are,
don't you? The flowers, I mean. They're forget-
me-nots. Well, Robert sendin' them makes them
mean, Forget-Robert-not . . . D'you see? It's a sort
of *message*. . . . Well, good-bye."

With that, he went out of the room, out of
the cottage and down the garden path to the road,
whistling loudly and untunefully in his relief at having
conducted a difficult and delicate interview to his own
entire satisfaction.

Miss Gaye sat gazing in front of her with a
stupefied expression.

Miss Petworth entered, twirling her spectacles.

"I see your suitor's gone," she said. "Won't you
unburden your heart to me?"

Miss Gaye looked at her long and hard. "I'll do
that all right," she said grimly, "but I want a good
stiff drink first."

*   *   *

William, however, had not yet finished his afternoon's work. As he reached the corner of the
road, he ran into Miss Rosalyn Abbot—a girl
of nineteen in whom, some weeks ago, Robert
had evinced unmistakable interest. It occurred to
William that here, too, he might put in a bit of spade
work. . . . It would be as well for Rosalyn to realise
that Robert was now completely out of her reach, so
that she should not introduce any complications into a
situation that he imagined he had reduced to a beautiful
simplicity. . . . He could not know, of course, that

Robert's interest in Rosalyn and Rosalyn's interest in Robert was as ardent as ever, but that Robert, learning wisdom from his previous affairs, was doing his best to hide this affair from the mocking eyes of his family. He could not know that the fatuous, faraway expression he had noticed on Robert's face when Gloria Gaye was mentioned had nothing to do with Gloria herself, that it was connected solely with the hours he had spent in the enclosed darkness of the cinema, with Rosalyn's hand in his, watching the tortuous melodrama of "Love in a Mist", and thinking how inferior was its heroine to the wonderful Rosalyn. He could not know that Robert had arranged to meet Rosalyn that evening and give her dinner at the Grand Hotel in Hadley.

"Hello, Rosalyn," he said.

"Hello," she said, looking at him disapprovingly.

Rosalyn did not like small boys, and certainly William was no pleasing object just now—his face streaked with paint and mud, his whole person freely sprinkled with forget-me-not seeds.

"What's that stuff you've got all over you?" she went on.

"Flowers," said William, brushing some of it off. "I've jus' been taking some flowers to Gloria Gaye from Robert."

"Some what?" said Rosalyn with ominous calm.

"Flowers," said William.

"Did you say flowers?" said Rosalyn.

"Yes," said William.

"To *whom?*"

"Gloria Gaye."

"You didn't say from *Robert*, did you?"

"Yes," said William.

"You've been taking flowers from Robert to Gloria Gaye?" said Rosalyn, speaking so slowly, and in so meaning a tone that each word seemed to form a separate sentence.

"Yes," said William, and added: "He's crazy on her. He wants to marry her."

"Oh!" said Rosalyn. "Oh, the *brute!*"

"Didn't you know?" said William, opening his eyes in a way that was meant to convey innocent surprise but that actually imparted a slightly imbecile expression to his homely face. "They're prob'ly goin' to get married quite soon now. Well, good-bye."

With that he turned on his heel and proceeded along the road, with Jumble at his heels, satisfied that he had displayed the utmost diplomacy and finesse in this interview, too.

Rosalyn stood looking after him, her lips set in a tight line, her eyes blazing, assuming the attitude that Rachel had assumed in "Fortunes of Rachel" when she heard of Harold's perfidy. Rosalyn, though distractingly pretty, was a girl of limited intelligence. She went to the pictures in Hadley twice a week, and on the intervening days moulded her life and emotions on those of the heroine she had last seen. The other week, sitting hand in hand with Robert, she had followed the fortunes of Rachel through their long and harrowing course to the final goal of happiness and marriage. It was during the second reel that the harpy Geraldine had stolen the weak but well-meaning Harold from Rachel, and Rachel, on first hearing the news, had stood like this—lips tightly set, eyes blazing. . . . Then she had controlled her emotion. Her lips had taken a wistful droop, her eyes had grown bright with unshed tears, as she made her way to Geraldine's flat, to plead with

her in tremulous passionate accents for Harold's heart.
Rosalyn went through this scene in her mind to be sure
she'd got it right and then, lips drooping wistfully,
eyes as bright as she could manage it, with unshed
tears, turned down the lane that led to Honeysuckle
Cottage.

* * *

"William!"

William wheeled round to see his mother just
behind him.

Mrs. Brown had gone home with the shopping
and was now on her way to the pillar-box to post a
letter.

"What *have* you been doing?" said Mrs. Brown,
regarding her younger son with horror.

"Nothin'," said William.

"You look simply *dreadful*."

"Do I?" said William, surprised. "I thought I
looked all right."

"Did you break the hall window?"

"No," said William with quiet enjoyment. "Robert
did."

"And what's this Hobbins tells me, about your
wanting to take flowers to a friend who's got
leprosy?"

"Oh that!" said William evasively. "P'raps I did
sort of say it. I didn't mean it. I jus' sort of said
it absent-mindedly. Have you seen Henry or Douglas?"

"No."

"Well, I'd better go'n' see what's happened to
'em. G'd-bye."

He proceeded on his way, leaving his mother
gazing after him helplessly.

Chapter 8

Ethel was sitting curled up in an arm-chair in the drawing-room, knitting a pullover for Robert's birthday present, with a leaflet of instructions open on the chair arm beside her.

Outside on the lawn was the empty deck-chair in which Robert had been sitting.

In the distance Hobbins pottered about in his herbaceous border. Over everything lay an air of peace and stillness.

"Knit twice into the first stitch," murmured Ethel, "knit seven . . . knit twice into the next stitch . . ."

"Hello, Ethel."

She turned her head to see Jimmy Moore standing in the open french windows.

Ethel had numerous admirers, but Jimmy Moore was the most persistent of them. And, though he had many faults, Jimmy was the one whom Ethel liked best. He was good-looking, sincere, dependable, and could generally be trusted to see the funny side of things. His chief fault was an incomprehensible streak of meanness. He had a good position, a reasonable salary, but he hated spending a penny more than was necessary. They had had words on the subject last time they met.

"Hello," said Ethel. "Repeat from star to last five stitches."

"You alone?"

"I seem to be," said Ethel. "Knit five . . ."

Jimmy came in rather uncertainly. They had parted on terms of chilly politeness, and he wasn't quite sure of his reception.

"Where is everyone?" he said, sitting down and trying to seem more at his ease than he was.

"Father's gone to golf, Mother's gone shopping, Robert's in his bedroom doing the cricket club accounts, it's Emily's afternoon out and I don't know where William is."

"What's happened to the hall window?"

"I don't know. William, probably. It's generally William that happens to windows in this house."

"Ethel," said Jimmy earnestly. "I want to talk to you. I never seem to get a chance to talk to you alone."

"One minute, Jimmy," said Ethel. "I must count. There's supposed to be a hundred and six stitches on the needle. One, two, three . . ."

Jimmy fidgeted impatiently till she had reached a hundred and two.

"Look here, Ethel," he broke in, "I've been so unhappy since I saw you last that I've hardly known what to do with myself. . . ."

"I only make it a hundred and four," said Ethel. "It may have been with you interrupting me. I shall have to do it again."

Jimmy got up and strode about the room, hands in pockets, brow drawn into a frown.

"Ethel," he said, when she seemed to have finished, "you surely know what you mean to me——"

"I make a hundred and three now," she said.

"You'd better count them yourself. You only keep on interrupting me when I try to count them."

Jimmy took the needles and, with an air of barely contained fury, counted the stitches. "There are a hundred and eight," he said. "Now listen, Ethel——"

"That's two more than there ought to be," said Ethel. "Either I've made a mistake or the pattern's wrong."

"Can't you put the darn thing away for a minute?" said Jimmy irritably.

"No, I can't," said Ethel. "It's for Robert's birthday, and it's next month, and it'll take me every minute of my time to get it finished . . . I'm a rotten knitter," she added with simple truth.

"Can't you knit and talk?" said Jimmy.

"I am knitting and talking."

"I mean, talk about something else than knitting. My grandmother can."

"It's probably socks, then," said Ethel. "Or scarves. You can with those. I'm not going to bother with those extra stitches. I'm just going to knit them in."

"Ethel, when I think of some of the things you said to me the last time we met . . ."

"I said you were mean," said Ethel. "You *are* mean . . . *Damn!*"

"What's the matter?"

"It says 'change to No. 8 needles' and I don't know whether we've got any . . . Jimmy, do look in that top drawer in the tallboy to save me getting up. There's a box full of needles there. There probably are some eights."

Jimmy went to the tallboy. His face wore a look of savage intensity.

"Just because I don't waste *pounds* on you like some of the men you know . . . Is this it?"

"Yes . . . *Pounds!* You never even waste a *halfpenny*. That's what makes you so dreary."

"*Dreary!*" echoed Jimmy (there was horror, indignation, and reproach in his voice), then, remembering the task on which he was engaged and thinking that the sooner it was over the better, went on: "How do you tell when they're eights?"

"There's a round thing with holes in the box," said Ethel. "See which fits into the hole with eight on. . . . Yes, dreary. I get sick of walking an extra mile because it's not worth a twopenny bus fare and not having tea out because it's a waste of money because we can get it at home, and going to the cheapest seat whenever we go out and——Stop jabbing them in like that. You'll break them."

"None of the darn things fit any hole at all. Now, listen, Ethel. . . ."

"Oh, bring them over to me. You'll only wreck every needle we've got in the house. . . . And it isn't because I want you to spend money on me. I'm willing to pay my share and I do. You know I do. But I hate doing things meanly. I don't get the kick you seem to get out of sordidness."

"Sordidness!" echoed Jimmy as if he couldn't believe his ears.

"All right, don't *throw* them at me. Now that's two under the settee. You'll have to get them out. . . . They're probably the eights, too."

"I think that's the first time I've been called sordid," said Jimmy. He tried to speak with dignity, but he was spreadeagled on the floor, groping with both hands under the settee. His voice was muffled and indistinct.

"Well, it probably won't be the last," said Ethel, "now I've come out into the open . . . I think that, if you go on long enough doing things meanly when you needn't, you get a sort of mean mind."

"What d'you mean, doing things meanly? . . . Here they are. Are they eights?"

"No, I've got the eights. They were in the box. And they *do* fit into the hole. Look!"

"They didn't when I tried them. And I asked what you meant by 'doing things meanly'?"

"I mean going up to London to a show and being expected to wait in a pit queue."

"An aunt of mine," said Jimmy coldly, "used to say that the front row of the pit was the best seat in the house."

"Well, we didn't even get that."

"And she used to say that you got more life and—and—amusement waiting in a pit queue than anywhere else."

"All right. Take your aunt next time. And don't talk any more till I've finished changing on to eight needles."

Jimmy leant back on the settee, his legs stretched out at length, his hands in his pockets, his scowling gaze fixed on his shoes.

"I've finished now," said Ethel. "What were you saying?"

"I wasn't saying anything," said Jimmy sulkily.

"Yes, you were. You were telling me about your aunt. Go on telling me about her."

"Ethel, do listen. I keep trying to talk to you and you won't let me start. You go on and on about that confounded jumper."

"It's not a jumper. It's a pullover. And it's a

complicated pattern. You should have come earlier.
If you'd come about half an hour ago I was doing a
whole stretch of thirty stitches, just pearl and plain."

"Well, I wasn't to know that, was I?"

"No. Well, go on talking. If I find I've missed any
with having to attend to the pullover, I'll ask you to
say it again."

"Ethel," he said. His anger was gone. He sounded
disconsolate and hurt and more than a little pathetic.
"Just because I—because I hope that sometime—when
I'm in a really settled position, I can ask you—I mean,
just because I'm trying to build up a little nest-egg for
the future when I—when we——"

"Jimmy, do stop pulling that hank of wool about.
You've no idea how difficult it is to get, and, if you
have to get some more, it's always a different
colour."

"Why?" said Jimmy, interested despite himself.

"I don't know. It just is."

"Ethel," said Jimmy, "I don't think you'll ever
know how some of the things you said last week
hurt me."

"Well, I don't think you'll ever know how it
hurt me to be expected to wait in a queue for
the cheap seats at a Hadley cinema and then go
and have supper at the cheapest place in the
town."

"It was all right, wasn't it? Fish and chips and
then an ice and coffee. . . ."

"And spills on the table-cloth and a waitress who
was only just not rude."

"What d'you mean, only just not rude? I never
noticed anything."

"I don't suppose you did. Anyway, I made up

my mind that I'd never go anywhere with you again as long as I lived."

"But—you are going to the tennis club dance with me, aren't you?"

"Yes."

"And the Dramatic Society picnic?"

"Yes . . . I fixed up both those before—last week. I've been asked by several people to go with them since, but I've refused."

"Who?" he said, scowling suspiciously.

"Oswald Franks and Gordon Franklin, and Ronald Bell. . . ."

"I can't think what you see in any of them," said Jimmy distantly. "Oswald Franks is a conceited idiot and Gordon Franklin is a half-wit and Ronald Bell"—he paused, searching for some flaw in Ronald Bell, and ended lamely—"well, he's got the rottenest service I ever saw."

"Tennis isn't everything," said Ethel.

"I know . . . Ethel——"

"Yes?"

"You know . . . there comes a time in a man's life when—I mean—when he turns his thoughts to—well, to marrying and settling down——"

"I don't see why you should," said Ethel. "You've got a very comfortable home. You've got a grandmother who can knit and talk, and an aunt who likes waiting in pit queues."

"I wish you'd let me speak for two minutes without interrupting."

"I wasn't interrupting," said Ethel calmly. "You said something and then I said something. I call that carrying on a conversation, not interrupting."

"Oh!" said Jimmy in desperation.

The telephone bell rang, and Ethel stretched out her hand to take up the receiver from the bureau by her chair.

"Yes? . . . Hello, Peter, how are you? . . . Good! . . . The tennis club dance? . . . I'm terribly sorry. I'm going with Jimmy Moore. . . . Yes, I'll see you at the club on Wednesday. . . . Good luck for the tournament. . . . Good-bye."

She put back the receiver. Jimmy sat glowering at her.

"What d'you mean, you're terribly sorry you're going with Jimmy Moore?" he said.

"Oh, do stop taking offence at everything I say."

"I'm not taking offence. I just didn't like the way you said it . . . Ethel. . . ."

Ethel went on knitting in silence.

"Ethel. . . ."

Ethel still went on knitting in silence.

"Ethel. . . ." There was a note of impatience in Jimmy's voice and he raised it a little.

"I'm sorry, Jimmy," said Ethel. "I was thinking about the pullover. I have to do two different rows alternately, and, if I do two of the same row together, the whole thing's ruined. Besides, I didn't think you just saying 'Ethel' needed any answer."

"I'm sorry if I seem unreasonable," said Jimmy stiffly, "but——"

The telephone bell rang again, and again Ethel lifted the receiver.

"Yes? . . . Oh, hello, Bruce. . . . The picnic? . . . No, I'm so sorry . . . I can't . . . I'm afraid I've fixed up to go with Jimmy Moore. . . . Yes, I'll be seeing you on Tuesday. . . . Good-bye."

She put back the receiver.

"Have you any objection to my saying, 'I'm *afraid* I've fixed up to go with Jimmy Moore'?" she asked. "You'd hardly expect me to say, 'I'm glad I'm going with Jimmy Moore,' would you?"

"No, I certainly wouldn't," said Jimmy bitterly. "Was that Bruce Monkton?"

"Yes."

"And where are you going to see him on Tuesday?"

"At the tennis club."

Jimmy gave a short mirthless laugh.

"Gosh, it's the funniest thing on earth to watch him trying to play a back-hander."

Ethel made no response.

"And he's putting on weight horribly."

Still Ethel made no response.

"Of course, the funniest thing of all is to see him play badminton."

"Knit four, purl two," murmured Ethel.

"Will you do me a favour, Ethel?"

"What is it?"

"Put that damned jumper——"

"Pullover."

"Pullover away for five minutes and let me talk to you."

Ethel glanced at the clock, folded up the pullover, put it on the bureau and lay back in her chair.

"Yes?"

Jimmy cleared his throat. "I want to begin, Ethel, by telling you how much——"

A series of thundering knocks resounded through the house.

"Heavens!" said Ethel. "That was the front door, wasn't it? I shall have to go and see who it is. Emily's out."

Jimmy groaned and dropped his head into his hands. Ethel went to the front door.

Henry stood there, holding an enormous bunch of magnificent carnations. He had been more fortunate—or perhaps more enterprising—than William. Having noticed a bowl of carnations on the hall table, he had merely waited till the coast was clear, then gathered them up and set out for the Browns' house. He did not know—nor would the fact have affected him deeply, had he known—that the carnations were prize blooms reared by his aunt and brought to his mother as a special present on the anniversary of her wedding-day.

"Come in, Henry," said Ethel.

Henry entered the drawing-room after her.

"These are for you from my brother John with his love," he said.

Jimmy ran his hands wildly through his hair. "Good God!" he said. "What did he pay for them?"

"When last I was in Hadley," said Ethel, "carnations like this were one and six each."

"Eighteen shillings," said Jimmy. "He must be mad!"

"Thank him for me very much, won't you, Henry?" said Ethel sweetly.

"Yes," said Henry, taking a seat opposite Ethel.

He had his message to deliver (he had learnt it by heart and was repeating it to himself now as he sat there), but he realised that it was a message that could not be delivered in the presence of a third person. The obvious course, then, was to wait till Jimmy Moore had gone. That might mean waiting a fairly long time, but he was prepared to wait a fairly long time. He had nothing else in particular to do.

Ethel had put the carnations down on the bureau. A long silence fell upon the company.

"You quite well, Henry?" said Ethel at last.

"Yes, thanks," said Henry. "Are you?"

"Yes, thanks," said Ethel.

"Are you?" said Henry to Jimmy, feeling that he should contribute a little social small talk to the occasion.

Jimmy grunted without removing his scowling gaze from the floor.

"Your mother will be expecting you back, won't she, Henry?" said Ethel.

"No," said Henry. "No, she's gone out."

Another silence fell. Henry was not embarrassed by it. He was silently repeating his message and waiting for Jimmy to go.

"Oughtn't you to be out in the fresh air on a day like this?" said Jimmy at last.

"No, I'm all right, thanks," said Henry. "I'm not partic'lar about fresh air. 'Sides," inhaling the air somewhat noisily through his nostrils, "smells quite fresh in here."

"Don't your friends want you?" said Jimmy.

"No, they're busy," said Henry.

"Doesn't—doesn't *anybody* want you?"

Henry considered this question conscientiously and answered simply, "No."

Jimmy groaned and dropped his head into his hands again.

"How sweet of John to have sent me the flowers!" said Ethel.

"It's quite all right," said Henry, vaguely polite.

Jimmy raised his head from his hands. "Get out," he said shortly.

Henry stared at him.

"Jimmy!" said Ethel.

"You heard what I said," said Jimmy to Henry. "Get out."

Henry rose uncertainly to his feet.

"I'd got a message from John to Ethel that I was to give her when no one else was there."

"This is too much!" moaned Jimmy.

"Come into the dining-room, Henry dear," said Ethel, and led him across the hall into the dining-room, closing the door.

"Well?" she said.

Henry cleared his throat and repeated his lesson, fixing his eyes on a spot about a foot above Ethel's head.

"He says he loves you with a most devouring passion. He says you're the apple of his life an' he's too shy to tell you himself an'—an' will you marry him?"

Ethel stared at him, and her blue eyes began to twinkle.

"P'raps you'd like some time to think it over," went on Henry kindly.

"I think I should," said Ethel. "I'd like a good long time."

"All right," said Henry. "I'll go away an' come back."

He heaved a deep sigh of relief at the successful accomplishment of his mission, went into the hall, snatched up his cap from the hat-stand, and took his leave.

Ethel returned to the drawing-room. Jimmy was standing by the bureau, his hands in his pockets, glaring down at the carnations.

He wheeled round as she entered. There was

an expression of grim disapproval on his face.

"I'm rather surprised to find you accepting expensive presents and—private messages, from a chap like that," he said.

"What's wrong with him?" said Ethel, sitting down and taking up her knitting again. "He's awfully nice. I've always liked him."

Jimmy began to pace about the room.

"I can't make girls out," he said. "You'd think they'd prefer a man who was careful and tried to save his money for—for—for——"

"A rainy day," supplied Ethel.

"Well, all right," he snapped. "I was just going to say it. A rainy day. But oh, no," sarcastically, "they prefer men who fling their money about, who make no provision for the future, who don't care whether their families starve or not. What sort of a husband will a man make who spends eighteen shillings on carnations every other minute? Tell me that."

"For one thing, he doesn't buy them every other minute," said Ethel, "and for another——"

"Ethel, don't let's quarrel," said Jimmy, sitting down by her. "Let's go back to where we were before that fiendish child came in. I was just going to tell you something I've been trying to tell you for weeks. You see——"

Another series of thundering knocks resounded through the house.

"That's the back door," said Ethel. "I'm sorry, Jimmy, but I must go. There's no one else in but Robert, and he's busy with his cricket accounts——"

Jimmy's groan was the most heartrending he had uttered that afternoon.

Ethel went to the back door. Douglas stood

there with an enormous pre-war chocolate box, tied up with blue ribbon. By means of a few pointed questions, he had elicited from his mother the fact that his father's most welcome present to her in their courting days, and indeed up to the time when the war put an end to such offerings, had been boxes of chocolates. And, though their contents had vanished quickly, she generally kept the boxes. The shelves in her wardrobe were full of them. She kept her handkerchiefs in them, her ribbons in them, her veils in them, her gloves in them. . . . Douglas had paid a surreptitious visit to her wardrobe and had chosen the biggest and the best, turning out a treasured collection of veils on to a shelf. He'd get the box back from William later, he assured himself, and replace the veils in it, before she discovered that it had gone. The contents proved a little more difficult, but, after all, he thought, even Ethel couldn't expect much in the way of sweets and chocolates these days. He found a couple of rather grubby acid drops in his pocket and put them at the bottom of the box. Then he filled the box with crumpled newspaper and on top he put two ancient monkey-nuts that he had found when turning out his play box, and quarter of a dried banana that his mother had given him that morning.

Then he put the lid on and took it round to the Browns' house.

"This is a present from my brother George," he said, handing it to Ethel.

"How kind of him!" said Ethel.

She opened the box and examined the contents.

"How *very* kind!" she said. "Won't you come in?"

"No, I don't think I will, thanks," said Douglas a little nervously, "but I'd gotter say somethin' with it. . . ."

He began to turn out his pockets. Douglas had a poor memory and knew that he'd have forgotten the speech William had told him to say, before he reached the Browns' house. So he had written it down on a piece of paper, meaning to refresh his memory just before he knocked. He'd done so, but he'd forgotten it again. . . .

"Here it is," he said, opening a slip of paper, " 'Maidstone on the Medway' . . . No, that's my g'ography . . . Wait a minute." He burrowed again in the chaotic confusion of his pocket.

"Don't bother, Douglas," said Ethel kindly. "I'll say it for you. You were to tell me that George loves me with a most devouring passion, that I'm the apple of his life and that he's too shy to tell me himself but he wants me to marry him."

Douglas stared at her. "Yes, that was it," he said. "How did you know?"

At that moment a hammering on the front door signified the return of Henry. Ethel went to open it.

"Have you finished thinkin' about it?" said Henry breathlessly. Then he caught sight of Douglas through the open kitchen door and his jaw dropped. "What's *he* doin' here?"

"The same as you," said Ethel. "Now I don't know what you kids are playing at and I don't care, but I'll give you just ten seconds' start and if you aren't out of sight by then . . ."

Already the two were in the road heading as fast as they could for open country.

Ethel smiled to herself and returned to the drawing-room, carrying the chocolate box.

"What's that?" said Jimmy.

"A present from George. Douglas has just brought it."

Jimmy gazed at it wildly.

"Heavens above! Where did he get it? How much did he give for it?"

"How should I know?" said Ethel.

"He's in some dirty black market racket," said Jimmy. "I shouldn't trust him an inch. No man who isn't a crook could get a thing like that these days. No man——"

The telephone bell rang again.

Jimmy flung himself on to the settee in an attitude of despair. "Some other blasted nit-wit wanting to take you to the tennis dance. Honestly, Ethel, I don't know what you see in all these——"

"Yes?" said Ethel, taking up the receiver. "Oh, good afternoon, Miss Abbot. . . . No, I'm afraid we haven't seen him. . . . He's not been here. . . . I'll let you know if he does. . . . I hope you find him soon. Good-bye."

She put down the receiver.

"It's that idiotic aunt of Rosalyn's. She's lost her cat again. Whenever it vanishes for half an hour, she begins ringing everyone up and combing the whole neighbourhood."

Jimmy had risen and was gazing fixedly at the chocolate box . . . then at the carnations . . . then at the chocolate box. Then he turned to Ethel. There was a set, rigid look on his face.

"Ethel," he said, "I'm going to say something and I mean what I'm going to say. I'm prepared to carry it through to the last detail." He paused and drew a deep breath. "Will you come up to London with me next Saturday and we'll have dinner at the Ritz and I'll take a box for some theatre?"

"Thanks, Jimmy," said Ethel. "I should simply hate it. I loathe going to London in the summer."

Jimmy ran his finger along his collar, and the rigidity of his expression relaxed.

"I'll tell you what, then," he said. "Let's go for a run in the car and then have dinner at the Grand Hotel in Hadley. You can't deny," he added, "that the Grand is the most expensive place in Hadley."

She didn't deny it.

"We'll have everything there is," he said recklessly. "We'll have the five shilling dinner and most expensive cocktail they've got and liqueurs with the coffee."

"I don't really like liqueurs," said Ethel.

"Well, I think they're a bit overrated myself," said Jimmy. Then, after a moment's thought, "And when you come to think of it they do an excellent dinner at the Red Lion for three and six."

Ethel burst out laughing.

"Oh, Jimmy, you are priceless," she said.

Chapter 9

Henry and Douglas did not stop to draw breath till they had nearly reached the old barn. Then, feeling themselves safe from pursuit, they slowed their progress to a walking pace, looking back occasionally to make sure that neither Ethel nor Jimmy was following them.

" 'S all right," said Henry. "No one's comin' after us. I didn't know you were goin' there."

"An' I didn't know you were goin' there," said Douglas aggrievedly. "You might have told me."

"Well, I thought you knew John was crazy on her. He always has been."

"So's George always been. An' now," disconsolately, "I bet there's no chance of marryin' either of them to her. I bet she'll marry that ole Jimmy Moore."

"He's got no manners," said Henry severely. "It's news to me," copying one of William's favourite expressions, "it's news to *me* that people that go callin' on other people with messages can get said 'Get out' to by other people that are only callin' on other people same as them an' that the house doesn't belong to. I don't mind," philosophically, "bein' said 'Get out' to by people that a house belongs to—I'm used to it—but *he'd* no right to say it."

Douglas, who was not interested in Jimmy Moore's

social lapses, continued the recital of his own grievances.

"She didn't even let me say anythin'," he grumbled.
"I bet I'd've found that paper if she'd given me
time."

William and Jumble were at the door of the
old barn, waiting for them.

"Well?" said William anxiously. "How did you
get on?"

"We didn't get on at all," said Douglas. "We
both went to Ethel an' she jus' sent us away. She
didn't even *answer*. Gosh! I wish I hadn't put those
acid drops in. I bet I never see them again."

"An' I bet I get in an awful row for takin' those
flowers," said Henry, for the memory of the action
that had seemed so necessary and reasonable at the
time was beginning to fill him with apprehension now
that tea-time and a return to the bosom of his family
loomed nearer.

"Oh, Ethel!" said William. "Dunno why you went
to *her*. She's the worst-tempered girl I've ever met.
Dunno what all those men *see* in her."

"She—*looks* sort of nice," said Douglas.

"I've seen her when she doesn't," said William
darkly.

"How did *you* get on?" said Douglas.

"All right," said William, casting a somewhat
optimistic eye back over the events of the afternoon.
"She didn't say she *wouldn't* marry him, anyway. An'
she took the flowers."

"What did you give her?"

"Forget-me-nots," said William. "Off the rubbish
heap. But there was quite a lot of blue left on them.
On some of them, anyway."

"Well, we don't seem to've got much done so far," said Douglas morosely. "Has anyone left a note wantin' a wrong rightin'?"

"No," said William, "I've looked."

"Doesn't matter what we try to do," said Douglas, "somethin' always goes wrong with it."

"Oh, shut up grumblin'," said William. "There's a lot of the day still left. I bet we do *somethin'*. Where's Ginger?"

"Dunno. *He's* jolly lucky havin' his brother fixed up to get married already."

"Makes you wonder whether a bike's worth it."

"It jolly well *is* worth it."

"Those monkey-nuts, too!" said Douglas gloomily. "I bet there was nothin' wrong with them. I've eaten things much older than that. I could easy have given it her empty. After all, it was a *box*."

"Here's Ginger."

Ginger was coming up the hill to the old barn, walking slowly, his face wearing a despondent expression.

"Hello, Ginger," said William as he reached them. "You're jolly lucky not bein' in this getting people married business."

"Well, I sort of am in it," said Ginger a little apologetically.

The four sat down on the grass by the barn door. Jumble took his seat with them, closing the circle.

"What d'you mean?" said William, pulling up a piece of grass and eating it.

"Someone once told me there was poison in the ends of grass," said Douglas.

"Well, I'd've died every day if there had been."

"You couldn't die every day. No one could."

"Oh, shut up. What d'you mean, Ginger?"

"Well, I thought I'd—sort of get my cousin Richard married."

"Why? What's he got to do with it?"

"Well, he's got a bugle."

"What's *that* got to do with it?"

"Well, he might give it me if he married."

"You've got a bike. Isn't that enough?" said William bitterly.

"No. I want a bugle, too. Richard lives next door and he hasn't any young brothers or anythin' an'—well, married people don't need bugles. I've never heard of a married person with a bugle."

"I don't suppose you've heard of everyone in the world. Why shouldn't married people have bugles?"

"I don't think their wives let them. Women don't like music. My mother's always sayin' that my mouth organ goes through an' through her head."

"Yes, there's somethin' in that . . ." said William slowly. "How did you get on?"

"Well," said Ginger. "I knew he was keen on this girl called Valerie Greyston, so I thought I'd take her somethin' same as you, an' say the same things you were goin' to say. An' I asked my mother what my father used to take her, an' she said fruit mostly. Grapes an' peaches an' things. Well, I couldn't get any grapes or peaches, 'cause I haven't any money, so I went to Mr. Netherby, you know, at the fruit shop——"

They nodded.

"He's jolly decent, you know. He often gives us things that are jus' a bit bad but not bad all over."

Again they nodded.

"Well, I asked him if he'd got anythin' an' he said

he'd got a pineapple that he was jus' goin' to throw out, 'cause it was rotten, but he fetched it an' showed it to me, an' it looked all right." He was silent as a mental vision of the pineapple came to him. "Well, you wouldn't've known from the outside that there was much wrong with it. Not *very* much, anyway. Anyway, you could see it had *been* a pineapple. An' the inside wasn't as bad as all that, 'cause I tried it. I've eaten worse things. . . ." He paused.

"Go on," said William.

"Well, I took it to her. It got a bit messed up on the way, 'cause I saw that ole cat of Miss Abbot's, an' I forgot it was a pineapple I was carryin' an' threw it at it, an' those fern things on the top got a bit broke up, but one of 'em stayed all right. It was only a bit bent, anyway. Anyway, I took it to her an' she came to her door and I said, 'This is from Richard with his love,' an' gosh! the way she carried on! Wouldn't even let me say those things you'd made up for us to say, an' I'd spent all the time on the way learnin' 'em. You'd've thought I'd murdered her, the way she went on."

"Ethel was nearly like that, too."

"There was nothin' wrong at all with parts of it," said Ginger. "Parts of it"—in a reminiscent and aggrieved fashion—"were as good as new."

"Well, we're not much nearer gettin' anyone married," said Douglas.

"Hello, William."

They looked up to see Violet Elizabeth standing by them.

"Go away," said William. "We're busy."

"Are you thtill righting wrongth?" said Violet Elizabeth, sitting down and edging her way into the circle.

"Never mind what we're doing. We don't want you."

"We had a perthon to lunth who wath talking about wrongth," said Violet Elizabeth. "Thee wath talking about people without hometh."

"Oh, yes, my father was talkin' about that this mornin'," said William. "It wasn't very int'restin'."

"But it muth be *thad* not having a home, William," said Violet Elizabeth.

"Might be fun," said Ginger. "They couldn't make you wash your hands, 'cause there wouldn't be a bathroom to wash them in."

"An' all your meals would have to be picnics," said Henry.

"An' they couldn't make you go to bed, 'cause there wouldn't be a bed to go to," said Douglas.

"But ith a *wrong*," said Violet Elizabeth earnestly. "You ought to do thomething about it."

"How can we?" said William irritably. "We can't *build* houses, can we?"

"Why can't we?" challenged Violet Elizabeth.

"We haven't got the right tools," said Ginger. "I've only got half a fretwork saw and a screwdriver."

"I've got a thing for taking the topth off bottleth," said Violet Elizabeth.

"Oh, shut up," said William. "You need bricks an' slates an' things. 'Sides, it takes *weeks* to build a house."

"Thith perthon wath thaying," said Violet Elizabeth, "that people who have got houtheth ought to take people who haven't got houtheth into their houtheth."

"Well, there's no room in our house," said Ginger. "My mother says you couldn't swing a cat in it."

"Ith cruel to thwing cath," said Violet Elizabeth.

"Yours is the only house here with a lot of rooms

in it," said William, referring to the spacious mansion
that Violet Elizabeth's father had purchased with the
proceeds of his much-maligned Digestive Sauce, "so,
if you want somethin' done, you can jolly well do it.
Anyway, I'm sick of rightin' wrongs. Let's go to the
woods an' practise trackin' each other."

They walked down the field to the lane in silence,
their minds busy with their grievances.

"I bet it would've been all right, if Douglas hadn't
come to Ethel's, too," said Henry. "I bet if I'd been
the only one . . . She seemed jolly pleased with those
flowers, an' she only wanted time to think it over. I bet
if Douglas hadn't come along, too, she'd've promised
to marry him." He sighed. "Why his brother's got to
get slushy over the same girl as mine . . .'

"I once read a book at school," said Ginger,
"about two men that were in love with the same
girl. A man called Shakespeare made it up."

"Let's write to him and ask him what to do,"
suggested William.

"We can't," said Ginger.

"Why not?" said William.

"He's dead," said Ginger. "Fancy not knowin'
that Shakespeare's dead!"

"Well, how was I to know?" demanded William.
"I can't know everyone's name that's dead, can I?
I bet there's a lot of dead people's names you don't
know."

"I bet I know more dead people's names than
you do."

"I bet you don't. I bet I——"

"Look!" said Henry, pointing down the lane.
"There's someone dead."

They looked down the lane. Stretched out on

the grass by the side of the road was a tattered, inert figure.

"He's not dead," said William.

"I bet he is."

"I bet he isn't. They don't let people die near the road like that."

"P'raps it's Shakespeare," suggested Douglas.

"We'll soon find out if he's dead," said William, slipping off his garter and picking up a pebble from the road.

The pebble landed neatly on the tramp's shin. He sat up, yawned, stretched and looked about him. No one was in sight, for the Outlaws had taken refuge in the ditch, dragging Violet Elizabeth with them. The tramp was obviously unaware that anything beyond the normal course of time and nature had caused his awakening. Slowly he untied a large handkerchief, took from it a slice of bread and cheese and, with an air of epicurean relish, began to munch it. The Outlaws craned their heads out of the ditch and watched him. He was gloriously unkempt, with straggling hair and beard, and small twinkling eyes in an incredibly dirty face. He had taken a battered straw hat from the ground beside him and set it at a jaunty angle on his tousled locks. They gazed at him in wistful admiration. . . .

Having finished his bread and cheese, he took out a large bone with a fair quantity of meat still adhering and set to work on it with the same suggestion of enjoyment as he had shown in the consumption of the bread and cheese. So absorbed was he that he did not notice the gradual approach of the Outlaws till he looked up to find them standing round him in a semi-circle.

"Hello, young gents," he said. "An' where are you off to this fine day?"

"To the woods," said William. "Where are you?"

"Anywhere an' everywhere," said the tramp jovially. "Wherever the fates may lead me."

"You can go jus' where you like, can't you?" said William.

"I can, young sir," said the tramp.

"An' you can do jus' what you like, can't you?"

"I can, young sir."

"He'th got holeth in hith coat, William," whispered Violet Elizabeth. "He mutht have got the moth in."

"Shut up!" said William.

"People aren't always makin' you wash your face an' brush your hair, are they?" said Ginger enviously.

"They are not, young sir," agreed the tramp.

"Gosh!" said Ginger. "It must be a wonderful life!"

"How d'you get to be one?" said William.

"Be one what?" said the tramp.

"A tramp."

"Tramp?" said the man, his merry twinkling eyes belying the indignation of his voice. "I'm a Knight of the Road, that's what I am."

"We're Knights, too," said Douglas. "We're Knights of the Square Table."

"We right wrongs," said Henry.

"Do you right wrongth?" said Violet Elizabeth to the tramp.

"Yes, little lady," said the tramp.

"What wrongth do you right?"

"Well, look here," said the tramp confidentially, "if a man's got too many rabbits in his field or chickens in his yard and I've got none, that's a wrong, ain't it?"

"Yeth."

"Well, I right it," said the tramp simply. "That's kindness to all concerned, ain't it?"

"Yeth," agreed Violet Elizabeth.

"How do you get into it?" said William again. "It sounds jolly fine."

"It's one of the best prerfessions there is," said the tramp, "but it's not easy to get into. I might say it's halmost impossible."

The Outlaws' faces fell, as visions of limitless freedom receded into the far distance.

"For one thing," said the tramp, "you've gotter pay a hentrance fee."

"Entrance fee?" said William.

"Now, listen," said the tramp. "You're lucky to have met me, 'cause I'm the head of the whole prerfession. No one can get into it 'cept through me. If you hadn't of met me now, you couldn't never of got into it."

"Gosh!" said Ginger.

"Once I let you into it, everythin's easy," went on the tramp. "You're one of us, then, see?"

They nodded solemnly.

"An', when you're one of us, we tell you the places you can sleep in for nothin', an' where you can get meals fer nothin'. An' we tell you the woods you can poach in an' the woods you can't." He stopped, looking at them with his merry twinkling eyes, and added, "But not even I can let you off the hentrance fee. I've took a oath never to let anyone in without the hentrance fee."

"How much is it?" said William.

The tramp glanced at them speculatively. "'Alf a crown each," he said.

Their faces were blank.

"Two shillings," he said.

"We've not got two shillings," said William.

"How much money have you got?" said the tramp.

"We haven't got any," said William.

"That's a pity," said the tramp, shaking his head. "That's a great pity, 'cause this is a chance wot may never come to you again all the rest of your lives." They gazed at him despondently. "But—listen now," he went on, "I've took a liking to you young gents, so I'm goin to do somethin' I've never done before."

"Yes?" chorused the Outlaws eagerly.

"I'm goin' to give you another chance. I'll come back 'ere to-morrer at the same time, an' if you've got the money by then, I'll let you in. P'raps," the merry twinkling eyes gave them another speculative glance, "you'll be able to get it by to-morrer?"

"We've *got* to get it," said William grimly.

"You may 'ave to wait a few years to *start*, of course," said the tramp, "but, once you've paid your hentrance fee, there'll be no difficulty. I'll be comin' along 'ere from time ter time ter keep in touch with you. But there's one condition."

"Yes?" chorused the Outlaws again.

"You mustn't tell no one what you want the two bob for. You've gotter give me your solemn oath that you won't tell no one. That's one of our strictest rules. If you tell anyone, the most 'orrible things'll 'appen to you an' I won't be able to stop 'em."

" '*Course* we won't tell," said William.

"You give me your solemn oath?"

"Yes," they said.

"Can Jumble be in it, too?" said William.

"Jumble?"

"My dog," said William, looking down at Jumble

who stood, head on one side, tail wagging, looking up at the tramp as if anxiously awaiting his fate.

"Oh, yes, 'e'll be all right," said the tramp. "Dawgs is useful. Poachin' an such."

"I'll start trainin' him poachin' at once," said William. "I bet I'll have him trained all right by the time we can get in it."

"Sure you will," said the tramp easily. " 'E looks a clever little dawg. 'E'll be a credit to us. So will you all." The Outlaws grinned with pride and pleasure.

The tramp picked up his bundle. "Well, I'll be gettin' on now. So long, young gents."

"So long," said the Outlaws.

"An' you've been jolly decent to us," said William. "*Thank* you."

"That's all right," said the tramp. "Don't forget the two bob, will you? I can't do nothin' without that."

"No, we won't."

They watched the tattered figure climb lightly over the fence that divided the lane from the wood and vanish among the trees.

"Gosh!" said William. "Fancy that happenin' to us!"

"I'd like to be jus' like him," said Ginger and added earnestly, "*Jus'*."

"If only we'd got that two shillings!" said Douglas.

"We'll get it," said Henry. "People *do* get two shillings. It happens every day. There mus' be some way of doin' it."

"Can I be a tramp, too, William?" said Violet Elizabeth.

"No. Tramps are men."

"I could be a lady tramp. There *are* lady trampth,

William. I've *theen* one. Thee looked *juth* like that one, but thee wath a lady."

"Anyway, he didn't want you. He only said 'gents'."

"I wouldn't be a nuithanthe if I wath a lady tramp, William," pleaded Violet Elizabeth wistfully.

"Yes, you would," said William. "You'd be a nuisance whatever you were. Anyway, I couldn't make you a tramp even if I wanted to and I jolly well don't. It's only him that can make you a tramp."

"He was jolly decent to us," said Ginger. "I wish there was somethin' we could do for him."

"William . . ." said Violet Elizabeth.

"Yes?" said William impatiently.

"He'th homeleth."

"What d'you mean, he's homeless?"

"He hathn't got a home."

"He doesn't want one, you idiot. He's a tramp. That's what tramps are for—not to have homes."

"But he *might* want one, William."

"Why should he?"

"He might want one in the winter. He might be cold and tired an' he might get influentha or meathleth or thomething."

"Well, it's not winter now, so it's no good talkin' about it."

"No, but we could tell him we'll give him a home in the winter. He might be pleathed. He might let me be a lady tramp."

They considered the idea, impressed by it, despite themselves.

"It would sort of show we're grateful to him," said Ginger.

"But we're jolly well not havin' *you* with us when we're tramps," said William to Violet Elizabeth.

"All right," said Violet Elizabeth loftily. "I'll be a lady tramp all by mythelf."

"Well, what house could we get for him?" said Henry thoughtfully.

"Thereth only ourth," said Violet Elizabeth with quiet triumph. "Thereth no room in any of your houtheth but ourth."

"I bet your mother wouldn't have him," said Douglas.

"Thee needn't know," said Violet Elizabeth. "There'th loth of thpare bedroomth, an' no one utheth them. Thee needn't know anything about it. We'd thow him the way to it, an' take him in hith mealth, an' then he could juth go away when he wanted to be a tramp again."

"Yes, an' once you've got someone into your house," said Ginger, "you can't turn 'em out. An aunt of mine once got someone into her house, an' she couldn't get them out. It's the lor."

"It's somethin' to do with the Magna Charta," said Douglas, adding hastily, as he saw Henry opening his mouth to challenge the statement, "but p'raps not much."

"An' it'd be rightin' a wrong," said Ginger. "We've not had much luck yet rightin' wrongs."

"Well, let's go'n' see if we can catch up with him," said William. "He can't have gone far."

They scrambled over the fence, Violet Elizabeth as usual bringing up the rear with a plaintive, "Wait for me," and hurried along the narrow woodland path.

A sudden bend showed him to them, ambling along in carefree fashion, his handkerchief bundle carried on a stick over his shoulder, a villainous-looking clay pipe between his lips.

"Hi!" called William.

The tramp turned round and waited for them, an expression of pleased surprise on his face.

"Well, you've not taken long," he said. "I will say that for you. I ain't got me receipt forms on me, but I'll book it to you in me mind."

"Book what?" said William.

"Yer two bobs." A slight cloud dimmed the brightness of the hairy, grubby countenance. "You—you 'ave brought 'em, 'aven't you?"

"Not yet," admitted William, "but we'll bring them to-morrow. What we wanted——" He hesitated, uncertain exactly how to express what he had to say.

"Yus?" said the tramp, looking down at the five earnest faces upraised to his.

"Well, you're—you're homeless, aren't you?" said William.

The tramp had recovered from his first disappointment. He was obviously not a man to brood unduly on any grievance. He chuckled. "You might put it that way," he said. "The trees an' ditches is my 'ome. I don't say," with a wink, "I ain't never been between four narrer walls, but the less said about that the better."

"You—you aren't int'rested in houses, are you?" said William tentatively.

The tramp lowered his voice confidentially. "Now, you've just 'it on the very thing I *am* int'rested in, young 'un."

"Oh," said William, relieved. "Well, we thought that p'raps in the winter if you were tired or—or——"

"Had meathleth," put in Violet Elizabeth.

"Shut up."

"Or mumpth," said Violet Elizabeth defiantly, "or chicken pokth."

"Shut *up*. Well, we thought that p'raps in the winter if you wanted to get into a house for a bit we could show you how to."

"Summer or winter," said the tramp, "I'm always ready to be showed how to get into a house."

"Wath your name?" said Violet Elizabeth suddenly.

"Hanything you like," said the tramp. "What's in a name, as the poet said. A rose by hany other name would smell as strong."

"Sweet," said Henry.

"Strong," said William firmly. "If *he* says it's strong, it *is* strong."

"All right," said Henry. "I only thought it was sweet," and, aware that he was in a minority, muttered in an undertone, "I still think it is."

"I'll call you Mithter Rothe," said Violet Elizabeth. "Ith a nithe name."

"O.K. by me, little lady," said the tramp.

"It's this girl's house that we're goin' to show you how to get into," said William. "We get into her garden gen'rally through a hole in the hedge, 'cause they've got a cross gard'ner. We get into most gardens that way, 'cause they've mostly got cross gard'ners. Could you manage to get through a hole in a hedge?"

"The 'ole I can't get through ain't bin invented yet, young 'un," said the tramp.

Certainly he manipulated the hole with unexpected nimbleness and followed the Outlaws through a winding path along a spinney that bordered the drive till they came in sight of the house.

"You can get up that pear tree that grows by the conservat'ry," said William, "an' in at that window. It's a spare bedroom, an' the window's always open. You could have a good rest in there any time you want. Would you like to try now?"

"That depends on circs," said Mr. Rose, a certain nervousness invading the geniality of his manner. "I was never one to force me company where I'm not wanted."

"There'th nobody there to mind, Mr. Rothe," said Violet Elizabeth. "My mother'th gone out an' there'th only Cook at home, an' thee thleepth in the rocking-chair in the kitchen all afternoon. Thee liketh the rocking-chair. Thee thayth ith thoothing."

"That's different," said Mr. Rose. "That's quite different, that is."

"I'll take you in," said Violet Elizabeth, leading the way to a side door that led from the garden into a small passage.

"You thtay here," she whispered, "an' I'll thee if thee'th athleep."

She tiptoed down the passage and soundlessly opened a door at the end. Rhythmic snores floated out. Soundlessly Violet Elizabeth closed the door and returned to the strange group, consisting of ragged tramp, four small boys and a dog, who, all poised for instant flight, were awaiting her in the doorway.

"Thee'th thtill finding it thoothing," she reported. "Come on in."

"I'd better leave Jumble outside," said William. "I'm trainin' him bein' quiet, but he's not quite learnt it yet. He's always thinkin' things are mice or rabbits."

He entered last and closed the door on Jumble. Jumble was accustomed to being left outside closed doors, but he liked to know what was going on. He stood there motionless, ears cocked, nose at the crack of the door, tail moving in an uncertain, rather anxious fashion.

"Ith thith way," whispered Violet Elizabeth, leading the curious procession up a flight of back stairs and along another passage.

"Thith ith the room," she said, opening a door.

They entered and looked round a spacious well-furnished bedroom.

"You can come an' retht here whenever you like," she said, "an' you can get out by the pear tree if you don't want my mother to thee you."

"I don't think I partic'ly want to meet your ma, some'ow," said Mr. Rose slowly. "No offence meant an' none taken, I 'opes?"

"Are you thy?" said Violet Elizabeth.

"That's right," said Mr. Rose. "I'm shy. Always 'ave been."

"Yeth, an' thee's a bit of a nuithanthe," said Violet Elizabeth sympathetically. "Thee'd be making you wath your fathe and bruth your hair."

"Shut up talkin' so much, Violet Elizabeth," said William sternly, then, turning to the tramp, "Well, you can come here whenever you want."

Mr. Rose was inspecting his new surroundings with interest. He went to the window and looked with a practised eye at the convenient means of exit. Then he turned to his hosts.

"That's a kind thought, young gents," he said. "A kind thought for a pore tired man . . . I think I'll 'ave a little rest now, if there's no hobjection."

"You didn't seem tired," said Henry.

"No," agreed Mr. Rose. "It comes on me sudden-like, an' I gotter rest or I don't know what'd 'appen to me."

"Have a rest on the bed," said William solicitously. "Gloria Gaye rests, too. Grown-ups get sort of tired jus' with bein' grown-up. I've often noticed it."

They stood there, obviously meaning to watch their protégé undergoing the process of recuperation.

"Yes, I will," said Mr. Rose, "but I've gotter be alone to rest. That's what my doctor said to me. He said, 'You've gotter rest, reg'lar, an' you've gotter be alone, or I don't know what'll 'appen to you'."

"All right," said William. "It's tea-time, anyway, so we've all got to go home. Well, we'll bring the two shillings to-morrow. That'll be all right, won't it?"

"Yes, that'll be all right," said Mr. Rose, trying the wardrobe door and finding it locked.

"An'—can I be a lady tramp?" said Violet Elizabeth anxiously.

"You can be what you like, little lady," said Mr. Rose, transferring his attention to the dressing-table drawers.

"Oo, thank you," said Violet Elizabeth, and then, "Are you looking for thomewhere to put your clothe while you retht?"

"That's right, little lady," said Mr. Rose.

"Well, you can put them in thith drawer, an', if you want anything from my motherth bedroom ith jutht neth door but one. She'th got *lovely* thilver brutheth an' thingth, if you want to bruth your hair, but I don't ecthpect you do. It lookth *nithe* like it ith."

"Oh, come on," said William, "an' let him have his rest. . . ."

They crept down the stairs and out of the side door, where Jumble greeted them ecstatically.

"Well, we've righted *one* wrong, anyway," said William, in a tone of deep satisfaction.

"ARE YOU LOOKING FOR THOMEWHERE TO PUT YOUR
CLOTHE WHILE YOU RETHT?" ASKED VIOLET
ELIZABETH.

"I'm going to be a lady tramp! I'm going to be a lady tramp!" shouted Violet Elizabeth exultantly, dancing about on one leg.

"Oh, shut up," said William. "Come on. Let's go home to tea. An' we've *got* to get those two shillingses."

Chapter 10

"Haven't you asked Jimmy to stay to tea?" said Mrs. Brown, as Ethel entered the kitchen.

"No," said Ethel. "I've had enough of him for one day. He's such a fool."

"I thought you liked him, dear," said Mrs. Brown, pouring hot water into the tea-pot.

"I do," said Ethel. "I like fools. I like them much better than sensible people. But one can have enough of them, and, for the time being, I've had enough of Jimmy."

"I see. Get the milk from the fridge, will you, dear?"

It was Emily's "afternoon out", and Mrs. Brown and Ethel were preparing the tea, treading carefully, as it were, on a knife's edge, for Emily was "touchy" about her kitchen and inspected every inch of it with gloomy suspicion after an absence, however short, during which the family had been left in charge.

"Is Robert in?" continued Mrs. Brown.

"No, he went out about five minutes ago."

"What about William?"

On weekdays Emily laid William's tea on the dining-room table, but Saturday tea was a vague elastic sort of affair and sometimes William did not come in for it at all.

"Put a cup for him. Perhaps"—hopefully—"he'll have it at Ginger's."

"One, two, three cups. . . . Did Pop say when he'd be back?"

"No. . . . It depends on how he's enjoying his game. Sometimes he finds that fourteenth hole a little depressing—or is it the fifteenth?—and he's glad to get home. . . . Put the tea-caddy back on the shelf, will you, dear? And do put it exactly where it was. You know what Emily is!"

"*Don't* I!" groaned Ethel. "If it's an inch wrong in one direction, we've messed up the whole kitchen and it'll take her weeks to get it straight, and, if it's an inch wrong in another, it means we're not satisfied with the way she keeps things and she gives us notice again."

"Yes, it's very difficult," sighed Mrs. Brown. "Here are the sandwiches, dear. Put them on the trolley."

"What does she do on her afternoons out?" said Ethel, putting the sandwiches on the trolley.

"I think she meets Mr. Heppleback, but she'd never admit it. . . . There! I think that's everything. . . ."

"Mother," said Ethel, beginning to push the trolley into the drawing-room, "William's up to something."

"Not again!" groaned Mrs. Brown. "We've forgotten the sugar. I'll bring it. How do you know?"

"I don't *know*," said Ethel, "but Henry brought me some flowers from John, and Douglas brought me a chocolate box from George this afternoon."

"How kind, dear!"

"And both made little speeches asking me to marry them."

"Marry Henry and Douglas?"

"No, marry John and George."

"How very odd! Mind the door with the trolley. You couldn't marry both, anyway."

"I wouldn't marry either. But I'm sure William's behind it."

"You shouldn't blame William for everything, Ethel. I'm always telling you that he means well."

"That's what makes him so dangerous. Anyway, I'm certain William's behind what happened this afternoon. Shall I pour out?"

"Please, dear. Well, you'd better ask him when he comes in."

"A lot of good that'll do. He'll put on that wooden look, and you might as well talk to a stone wall. Here he is," she added as William, tousled and whistling, came up the garden path.

He did not enter by the french window, but, going round to the front door, placed his cap on the deer's head, putting it low over its eyes and taking a scarf of Robert's to tie on its mouth as a mask, making it look rather like an ineffectual hold-up gangster.

"I'm not late for tea, am I?" he said as he entered.

"No, dear," said Mrs. Brown. "Is that red paint on your face?"

William threw his mind back over the events of the day, frowning thoughtfully.

"It might be," he admitted, "but I don't see how it could be. I did use red paint once, but it was a long time ago. I should have thought it'd've worn off by now. Anyway, I don't see how I got it on my face. I only wrote with it."

"*Wrote* with it?" said Mrs. Brown. "Why on earth did you write with red paint? Couldn't you find any ink?"

"It was better than ink for what I wanted."

"What did you want?"

"Oh, nothin' much," said William. "I mean it was somethin' jolly important, but——"

"What isn't red paint seems to be mud," said Ethel, looking with unconcealed disgust at what she could see of her young brother's features.

"Mud?" said William, frowning and again casting his mind back over the events of the day. "Oh, yes, I did get into a bit of mud, too, but that was a long time ago, too, an' it wasn't near my face, either, so I don't see——"

"What were you doing in mud, William?" said Mrs. Brown. "It's a perfectly dry day."

"Well, I went for a bit of a walk," said William vaguely, "an'——Wait a minute, I'll clean it up."

He took out his handkerchief, looked at it and hastily thrust it back into his pocket. "All right, I'll go an' wash," he said with an air of one offering himself for sacrifice.

"Mother, did you *see* his handkerchief?" said Ethel, when the sound of his footsteps had died away.

"No, dear. I was cutting the cake."

"It was indescribable," said Ethel.

Mrs. Brown rose and went to the foot of the stairs.

"Put that handkerchief into the soiled-linen basket, William," she called.

"Did you see it?" called William.

"No."

"Oh, well, it's not too bad. There's a bit of clean left at one corner, an'——"

"Put it into the soiled-linen basket at once and get out a clean one."

"All right," said William regretfully.

His handkerchieves, when they had reached a certain

stage of degradation, became trusted friends and allies to him. A clean one wore a superior, supercilious air, and seemed to play its part reluctantly in his various activities.

He came down after a few minutes, face and hands washed, hair driven into a wild spiky circle round his face.

"You haven't brushed your hair, William," said Mrs. Brown.

"Sorry," said William, smoothing it back with a hand that left no trace of its passing.

"Well, never mind now," said Mrs. Brown resignedly.

"Can I have my tea, please?"

"Yes. Wouldn't you like to take it into the dining-room and have it at the table?"

"No, thanks," said William. "I'm all right in here."

"Well, take what you want from the trolley and go and sit on the step of the french window, so that your crumbs fall outside, if possible."

Mrs. Brown had learnt by experience that tea in the drawing-room could be reduced by William to a sea of crumbs extending from end to end of the carpet.

"William," said Ethel, when he had carried a laden plate across the room with only a few minor casualties and seated himself on the step of the open french window.

"Yes?" he said guardedly.

"What were Henry and Douglas up to this afternoon?"

He turned an expressionless face to her.

"I wasn't with them," he said innocently. "How c'n I know what people are up to when I'm not with 'em?"

"Did you know they were coming here?"

William wrinkled his brow thoughtfully.

"Well, it's difficult to remember what people tell you an' what they don't. Sometimes they tell me what they're goin' to do an' sometimes they don't. I've not got a very good memory an'——"

"Oh, all right," snapped Ethel, "you needn't go on with it. I knew you were up to some trick. And *look* at those crumbs you're making on the parquet. Hundreds of them."

William looked. "I bet," he said judicially, "there's not even a hundred. I bet there's not more than fifty. I bet there's not even fifty. I'll find out. One, two, three——"

"Oh, for heaven's sake, don't *count* them. Clear them up."

"All right," said William, clearing them up by the simple process of collecting them on a damped finger and putting them into his mouth.

"William, you are *disgusting*."

"I'm not," said William, hurt and surprised. "It's a jolly good cake an' I don't want to waste any of it. An' it's a clean floor, isn't it? Emily cleans it, doesn't she? It's news to me that Emily doesn't clean floors an'——"

"Be quiet, William," said Mrs. Brown. "Get on with your tea without talking so much, and try not to make so many crumbs. . . . Oh, I got you some elastic, Ethel. They had some at the post office."

"Thanks so much," said Ethel.

"That new man from the Manor was there," went on Mrs. Brown.

"Ole Monkey Face," put in William indistinctly.

"Don't talk with your mouth full, William. He

was terribly rude to me. Pushed past me to get to the counter and nearly knocked me over. He was asking if there was a letter for him, care of the post office."

"What does he want to have letters sent care of the post office for?"

"I don't know. He's a horrible-looking man."

"Yes," sighed Ethel.

Ethel was in no need of local admirers, but there was a hidden streak of romance in her nature, and, when she had heard that a new tenant, male and unattached, was expected at the Manor, she had hoped for something very different.

"You won't call, will you?" she said.

"Certainly not," said Mrs. Brown. "It wouldn't be any use, anyway. The Vicar called, and, though he saw someone at a window, nobody answered the door. The man's evidently very unsociable."

"Perhaps he's a writer," said Ethel.

"P'raps he's found a gold mine in the earth underneath his house," suggested William, "an' he doesn't want people to know."

"Don't be silly," said Ethel. "He seems a very unpleasant specimen, anyway."

"He may be very nice *really*," said Mrs. Brown, who always tried to see the best in people. "One shouldn't pass judgment. He may have had a very unhappy life or—or—well, he may have had an unhappy life."

"He looks more as if he gave other people unhappy lives," said Ethel, rising and taking up her tea-cup. "I think I'll go into the garden and carry on with my sunbathing. Will you kindly allow me to step over your al fresco meal, William?"

"Yes," said William, moving to one side. "An',

if what you said means makin' crumbs, I've hardly made any since those others, 'cause I'm eatin' them soon's I make 'em. Only one of 'em tasted a bit of floor."

Ethel recoiled in horror, uttered a sound expressive of supreme disgust and, going out to the deck-chair that Robert had set up, lay back in it, raising her face to the sun and closing her eyes.

"May I have another piece of cake, please, Mother?" said William.

"Just one, dear, and then no more after that," said Mrs. Brown.

She had finished her tea and taken up her mending, putting her work-basket on the chair beside her. At the moment she was running her fist down one of William's socks. Meeting with no impediment, it ran out of the end of the leg through one of the largest holes that even William had ever made.

"*William!*" groaned Mrs. Brown.

"What am I doin' wrong now?" said William in a slightly aggrieved tone. "I'm only sittin' qui'tly havin' my tea."

"*Look* at this hole!"

"Oh, that!" said William, looking at it.

"I don't know *why* you go through your stockings like this."

"P'raps it's Latin," said William, after a moment's thought. Mrs. Brown considered this explanation in silence.

"How do you mean, Latin?" she said at last.

"Well," explained William, "you see all this Latin I've got to learn mus' make my brain jolly heavy, an'—well, you carry your brain on your feet, don't you, same as the rest of your body, an', if I stopped learnin' Latin, my brain wouldn't be as heavy as what it is now, an'—well, I shouldn't go through my stockings so much. Can I stop learnin' Latin?"

"No, dear," said Mrs. Brown, "and don't talk such nonsense."

William sighed. He hadn't really hoped for anything else. Between himself and the Latin master lay a long and bitter enmity. He had tried various ruses to induce his father and mother to let him stop learning Latin but none of them had worked.

There was another silence. William, having polished off a fairly satisfying tea, was now turning his thoughts to the chief business of the day, and that was to obtain the two shillings for his entrance fee into the tramp profession. He decided to try direct methods first.

"Will you give me two shillings, please, Mother?" he said.

"Certainly not," said Mrs. Brown.

"Will you give me *some* money, then? I haven't any at all."

"What have you done with your pocket-money?"

"Spent it."

"Well, if you hadn't spent it, you'd still have it, wouldn't you?"

William considered this statement, trying to find a flaw in its logic.

"I might have lost it," he said at last.

"Well, you didn't, William, so don't talk such nonsense. What do you want the two shillings for?"

"Oh—jus' somethin'."

"If you save up your pocket-money for the next four weeks, you'll have two shillings."

"Yes, but it'll be too late then."

"Too late for what?"

"Oh . . . jus' somethin'."

"Honestly, I don't know what to do with it," said Mrs. Brown, looking helplessly at his hole. "I wish you could wear leather socks."

"Well, why couldn't I?" said William, interested despite his other preoccupations. "I'd *like* to wear leather socks. Couldn't you get a piece of leather and cut it up into slices and knit them?"

"No, dear, of course I couldn't. If you've finished your tea, bring your things over to the trolley. I wish I could even patch them."

"Why don't you? I'd like 'em patched."

"You can't with socks. Do be careful of that knife, William. . . . *There!*"

"Why can't you with socks?" said William, picking up the knife.

"The wool would all run out. Mind! There's jam on that spoon . . . oh *dear!*"

"Where would it run out?" said William, picking up the spoon.

"Oh, do stop talking about it, dear," said Mrs. Brown wearily. "Wouldn't you like to go out into the garden?"

"No, thanks," said William, standing by her chair. "I like bein' in here talkin' to you. . . . Would you like me to wash up?"

"No, thank you, dear."

"Tell you what I'll do," said William with an air of reckless generosity. "It's Emily's afternoon out, so I'll help you. I'll wash up for you an' I'll only charge you sixpence. An' I'll polish the silver for you an' I'll only charge you sixpence. An' I'll set the dinner-table for you an' I'll only charge you sixpence. An' I'll peel the potatoes for you an' I'll only charge you sixpence for that, too. An' I'll *give* you cleanin' a window. Any you like. I'll throw it in. There! That's a bargain."

"*No*, William!"

"All right," said William gloomily, plunging his hands into his pockets.

"I wish you'd stand out of my light, dear."

William stood out of her light and tried to think of another method of approach.

"Mother. . . ."

"Yes, dear?"

"How much would it cost you to have me trained for a profession?"

"What profession, dear? Leave those scissors alone, William. You'll only do some damage with them. You always do."

"Sorry . . . Well, say, a doctor?"

"You'd have to work much harder at school than you do and be much cleaner and tidier before you could be a doctor."

William sighed.

"Yes, but we're not talkin' about that. An' I once saw a doctor that didn't look all that tidy. It was Dr. Bell, an' he'd got his overcoat buttoned on the wrong buttons."

"Perhaps he was coming from a night case."

"P'raps he was, only it was in the afternoon, but how much would it be?"

"Oh, several hundred pounds, I suppose," said Mrs. Brown vaguely.

"Well, I won't be a doctor," said William, as if making a dramatic renunciation.

"I never thought you would, dear," said Mrs. Brown. "I can't imagine you one. Don't fidget with those cotton reels. You'll only get them all in a tangle."

"Sorry . . . But I'll have to be *something*, won't I?" said William patiently, "an' you'll have to pay a lot of money to get me into it."

"I'm afraid so," said Mrs. Brown, "if we ever do."

"Well," said William, "I'll let you off all those hundreds of pounds, if you'll give me two shillings now."

"Don't be so silly, William, and leave that bias binding alone."

"Sorry . . . I'm not bein' silly. I've got a profession that you only need two shillings to get into, an' if you'll give me this two shillings——"

"*No*, William . . . Now go into the garden, dear."

"All right," said William dejectedly.

He went into the garden, muttering to himself.

"Won't even pay two shillings to get her own son into a profession. . . . Won't . . ."

He stopped. Ethel was still in the deck-chair. William looked at her speculatively, then approached her, standing on the rung of the deck-chair and resting his arms on the bar at the top.

"Hello, Ethel."

Ethel didn't answer.

"Ethel. . . ."

"I wish you'd stop breathing down my neck," said Ethel.

"Sorry . . . Ethel, would you like to do something about my future?"

"I'd like to do a lot about your future," said Ethel grimly, "and get off my chair. You'll have the whole thing down in a minute, and it won't be the first time—fidgeting about like that."

"Sorry . . . Would you like never to see me again? After a few years, I mean."

"Why must I wait? Get *off* the chair, William."

"Sorry. I forgot. I jus' got on it again without thinkin'. . . . Well, if you'll give me two shillings now you'll never see me again. After a few years, I mean. I'm goin' to get into a thing I can't tell you about 'cause it's a secret, but I'll be settled for life, if you'll give me two shillings now."

"I don't know what you're talking about," said Ethel, "but you won't get two shillings out of me, so you may as well stop trying. . . . And do stop hanging over me and breathing on me."

"All right," said William.

He went to the garden seat and took up a model aeroplane that he had made (not very skilfully) the day before. Once more raising her face to the sun and closing her eyes, Ethel resumed her sunbathing.

"I forgot I'd left this here," said William, examining it. "It's a jolly good one . . . I say, Ethel, I'll make you one like this for two shillings if you'll pay for the parts."

"What on earth should I want with it?" said Ethel.

"You could—you could give it me for my birthday present," said William.

She received the suggestion in silence.

"If you'll give me two shillings now," said William, "I'll make it to-morrow."

That suggestion, too, she received in silence.

"It's a jolly good one," said William again. "It goes a long way if you give it a good throw."

He demonstrated by giving it a good throw. It sailed through the air and descended on Ethel's nose.

She screamed and sat up.

"I'm sorry, Ethel," said William. "I didn't mean

it to do that. It must have got caught by the wind or somethin'."

"It speaks volumes for my self-control, William," she said slowly, "that you are still alive and walking the earth. I shouldn't bank on its going on too long."

She took up her tea-cup and went indoors.

William put the aeroplane back on the seat and followed her.

"I've been trying to rest in the garden with William there," she said. "That's a good joke, isn't it? . . . Is there any more tea?"

"It's a little weak," said Mrs. Brown. "William, I wish you'd stop worrying people."

"I like it weak," said Ethel. "You might as well ask the earth to stop going round."

"Well, I like that!" said William, aggrieved. "I was only showin' how my aeroplane worked. It wasn't my fault the wind blew it on to her. An' I've never believed that stuff about the world goin' round. We'd drop off it if it did. Stands to reason we would. Well——"

"Here's Father," said Ethel, glancing out of the window.

There was the sound of the opening and closing of the front door.

"I hope he's enjoyed his game," said Mrs. Brown.

Ethel craned her neck to look into the hall.

"He hasn't. He's taking William's cap off the deer's head."

Mr. Brown entered. He hadn't enjoyed his game.

"Who's broken that hall window?" he said.

"Robert," answered William promptly.

"I'll make some more tea, dear," said Mrs. Brown.

"Don't bother," said Mr. Brown. "What on earth was the fool doing? And it *would* happen on a Saturday.

"HAVE YOU BEEN USING YOUR GARTER FOR A CATA-
PULT AGAIN, WILLIAM?" SAID MRS. BROWN.

Now we can't get it mended till Monday, I suppose." He
glanced at his younger son. "Must you go about with
your stocking hanging right over your shoe like that?"

William looked down at his stocking and began
to rummage in his pockets.

"Have you been using your garter for a catapult
again, William?" said Mrs. Brown.

William went on rummaging.

"Your mother is speaking to you, William," said
Mr. Brown.

William rummaged in the last pocket and triumphantly brought out the garter that he had slipped
into it after awakening the tramp. He began to draw
it on to his leg.

"How did it get into your pocket?" said Mrs. Brown.

William apparently did not hear. He was engrossed
in the correct adjustment of his stocking.

"William!" said Mr. Brown.

William raised his eyes to his father's, and the
blank look closed over his face.

"I must've sort of put it in absent-mindedly,"
he said. "I'm always doin' things absent-mindedly.
Everyone does things absent-mindedly sometimes. I
once heard of a man who——"

"That'll do," said Mr. Brown shortly. "Go out
and play."

William went into the hall and opened the front
door. Hearing his name, he stopped for a moment,
scowling, to listen.

"You should have seen him when he came in,"
Ethel was saying. "He looked like a young tramp."

The scowl cleared from his face, and a blissful
smile enveloped it as he went down the path to the
gate and out into the road.

Chapter 11

Miss Gloria Gaye's rest cure was proving heavy going.

Almost immediately after William's departure the Vicar had arrived. The Vicar was no film fan. He never visited the cinema. Nor was he an admirer of Miss Gloria Gaye. He disliked her—and disliked her intensely—on sight. But he was a man of one idea, and that one idea was the Church Restoration Fund. He made it his duty to visit every person in the neighbourhood who, he had reason to believe, was possessed of surplus wealth, and to divert as much of that surplus wealth as he could to his Church Restoration Fund. Film stars, he gathered from what he had heard and seen in the papers, were possessed of considerable surplus wealth. They lived in an atmosphere of private swimming-baths, expensive jewellery that was always being stolen, secretaries, divorces (which cost money quite apart from the moral questions involved), and visits to the South of France, where they wore sun-spectacles and very little else. Probably even the sun-spectacles were expensive. . . . Therefore the Vicar, after much thought and much wrestling with a personal disinclination for his job, had decided to call on Miss Gloria Gaye and ask her for a contribution to the Church Restoration Fund.

The battered (he was an execrable driver), non-descript-coloured (it had once been brown) car drew up at the door of Honeysuckle Cottage, and Miss Gloria Gaye, who had set Miss Petworth to work on her fan mail upstairs, opened the door to him in person. They inspected each other without enthusiasm.

"Miss Gaye?" said the Vicar.

"Yes," said Miss Gaye. "Do come in."

He introduced himself and followed her into the little sitting-room. Then he sat down and cleared his throat. He was aware, of course, that he couldn't plunge into the Church Restoration Fund straight away, that he must lead up to it by a certain amount of social small talk.

"You're enjoying your stay here, I hope?" he said.

"Yes, thank you," said Miss Gaye.

"You work in films, I believe?" went on the Vicar.

"Yes," said Miss Gaye distantly, not liking his way of putting it.

The Vicar beat a tattoo on the arm of his chair with his fingers, trying to think of something to say about films. Then he brightened. Though he never went to the pictures of his own accord, he had once visited relations in Sheffield, who had taken him to the local cinema as part of the scheduled entertainment.

"I once saw a film in Sheffield," he said.

"Did you?" said Miss Gaye.

"It was some time ago," went on the Vicar, "and I forget many of the details, but it was, I remember, a strong and not wholly uninteresting story."

"I'm so glad," said Miss Gaye.

"As far as I can remember," said the Vicar slowly and thoughtfully, leaning back in his chair, joining the tips of his fingers together, and gazing into the distance, "the story turned chiefly on the activities of a criminal who turned out in the end not to be a criminal at all."

"Did it?" said Miss Gaye.

"It was the man's brother who was really a criminal," went on the Vicar, struggling to dispel the mists of time that stood between him and the long and wearisome afternoon he had spent in the Sheffield cinema, "and the man's brother had been taken seriously ill on the eve of one of his coups."

"His what?" said Miss Gaye.

"His coups," said the Vicar. "The man was summoned to his sick-bed and——"

At this moment there was another knock at the door, and Miss Gaye went to answer it, returning in a few moments with a reporter from the *Hadley Observer* at her heels. He was a small, thin, wiry man, accustomed to extract from each minute the full fine flavour of each of its sixty seconds. He had just come from a cricket match over at Marleigh and was due at a Young Liberal Association meeting in half an hour's time. Meantime, he meant to extort from Miss Gloria Gaye an interview, a photograph, and the promise of a personal appearance at the Hadley Cinema next Saturday evening.

The Vicar looked at him coldly and greeted him shortly. He thought that the reporter, having seen his car at the door (everyone within a radius of fifty miles or so had cause to know his car), should have deferred his visit till later. Moreover, he was annoyed with the *Hadley Observer* for not printing the last letter he had sent them on the subject of the desecration of the countryside at the hands of visiting trippers.

It was the third letter he had sent them on the

same subject within a few months, and even in the same letter the Vicar was apt to repeat himself, but he thought they should have printed it.

"Now, Miss Gaye," said the reporter briskly, sitting down opposite the Vicar and returning his greeting as shortly as it was given. "I won't beat about the bush. I represent the *Hadley Observer* and I've come for an interview."

Miss Gaye looked at him. She was a film star but only just, and she wasn't sure that she wanted to figure in small town local papers. The publicity of small town local papers was of a dubious nature. It stamped one, as it were. "Poor old Gloria!" she heard the more ill-natured of her friends saying. "Fancy coming down to that!"

She smiled at him sweetly.

"I've come here for a rest cure, you know," she said. "One gets so wearied of interviews and photographs and that sort of thing."

"Exactly," said the Vicar. "Miss Gaye shouldn't be pestered. . . . Well, this particular coup was to take place in a large country house."

The reporter stared at him.

"He's telling me about a film he once saw," explained Miss Gaye.

"Oh," said the reporter. "Now, just a short one, Miss Gaye." He whipped out a note-book. "Half a dozen questions or so. I could answer them for you myself, of course, but it would be more satisfactory for our readers if——"

"Perhaps I ought to have told you earlier," said the Vicar, "that the brothers were twins."

"Now, what was the name of the film in which you made your name?" said the reporter.

"Really," said Miss Gaye coyly, "I don't think——"

"In order to save his brother's life," said the Vicar, sticking to his guns, "this man promised to take his brother's place in this coup—this jewel robbery."

"Now don't pretend that it's so long ago that you can't remember," said the reporter.

Miss Gaye gave her famous musical trill of laughter, but there was a faint edge to it. Things like that should not be said even as jokes. . . .

"There was a love interest, of course," said the Vicar, "but I forget the details."

"I think it was 'Mud in Your Eye'," said Miss Gaye.

"Mud in my——" said the Vicar, startled.

The reporter made a note in his note-book.

"You can leave the rest to me, Miss Gaye," said the reporter. "Now, about a photograph. . . ."

"Well, I don't really know," said Miss Gaye, hedging and remembering what photographs in small town local newspapers made one look like. "I've never been one for publicity, you know."

The reporter made another note in his book.

"The man was captured," said the Vicar, "and there was rather an unconvincing court scene, in which, as far as I can remember, the judge wore a barrister's wig."

"Well, perhaps he *was* a barrister," suggested Miss Gaye, mildly interested.

"Just a *small* photograph," pleaded the reporter.

"He got off," said the Vicar, "because it turned out that the jewellery hadn't been stolen, after all."

"I think I shall get my photograph, shan't I?" said the reporter archly.

"My secretary——" said Miss Gaye, relenting.

"Good! And just a *short* appearance at the Hadley

Cinema on Saturday . . .? Just a *short* one?"

"I rather think it was some priceless old manuscript,"
said the Vicar, "and not jewellery at all."

"To give limitless pleasure to the people of Hadley?
To give them something to remember for the rest of
their lives?"

"Strange how it is all coming back to me," said the
Vicar, "after nearly twenty years, it must be. . . . You
didn't see the film yourself, by any chance, did you,
Miss Gaye?"

"No," said Miss Gaye coldly.

"You won't actually *refuse*, will you, Miss Gaye?
You wouldn't be so cruel as that? Think of all the
little children of Hadley being able to say to their
grand-children in after years that they'd *seen* Miss
Gloria Gaye herself. Herself, in person. . . . Ah! I see
I've won the day." He smiled, looked at the clock, shut
up his note-book and rose to his feet. "Well, I won't
keep you any longer. I'll write up the interview and I
assure you, Miss Gaye, it will do you full justice. *Full*
justice. I'll send round for the photograph later this
evening, and I'll give the glad news to the manager
of Hadley Cinema. Ah, there'll be joy in a hundred
hearts next Saturday."

"Or was it bullion?" said the Vicar suddenly. "I
have a very bad memory, but I'm coming more and
more to the conclusion that it wasn't jewellery."

"What's the population?" said Miss Gaye, still
pondering on the "hundred".

"I should have said *thousands*," said the reporter,
seeing her point and making for the door. "No, don't
trouble to show me out. I know my way. And thank
you a million times."

He shut the front door, took his bicycle and pedalled

hastily off to the Young Liberal Association.

Miss Gaye and the Vicar were left alone. There was a long silence. The Vicar was still frowning thoughtfully and gazing into space.

"I hope," he said, "that I didn't give you a wrong impression of the character of the brother who took his twin brother's place?"

"No, I don't think you did," said Miss Gaye.

"He was essentially a law-abiding citizen."

There was another long silence. During the silence the Vicar decided that he had wasted enough time on social small talk and could come straight to the subject nearest his heart—the depredations of the death-watch beetle on the wooden parts of the church fabric and the urgent need of further contributions to the Church Restoration Fund.

Now the Vicar was a man who took for granted that other people could follow the mental processes of his swift transitions of thought.

He broke the silence, speaking slowly and impressively.

"The beetle," he said, "has now invaded the stalls."

He always referred familiarly to his choir stalls as "the stalls".

Miss Gaye stared at him.

"I beg your pardon?" she said.

"The beetle," repeated the Vicar more distinctly, "has now invaded the stalls".

Miss Gaye's thoughts went wildly round in circles. She repeated the words to herself . . . "The beetle has now invaded the stalls." What did he mean? He obviously meant something. People—even this man—didn't say things that meant nothing, not in that tone of voice, anyway. And for no particular reason the idea came to her that she was being blackmailed. She was fast approaching the degree of respectability necessary to stardom, but she had not led an altogether blameless life.

"Beetle". . . . She had once known a short dark man with very bushy eyebrows. "Stalls". . . . She had once been a musical comedy actress in a small way. . . . Perhaps he wasn't a clergyman at all. . . .

Again he broke the silence.

"The screen," he said, "is beyond hope, but the gallery may yet be saved."

Miss Gaye continued to stare at him like a fascinated rabbit. "Beetle" . . . "stalls" . . . "screen" . . . "gallery". It was a code, of course. A sort of blackmailer's code. They daren't say a thing straight out in so many words or they'd have the police after them. Probably all that rigmarole about bullion and barristers' wigs meant something, if only she knew what. . . . Of *course* he wasn't a clergyman. He was a cunning and desperate blackmailer. There'd been one in the last picture she'd acted in. . . .

She tried to fit the words into various incidents of her life that she would not wish to be divulged. What was the "screen" that was "past hope"? What was the "gallery" that might "yet be saved"? She had a vague—a very vague—idea what he meant by the beetle in the stalls. . . .

He was speaking again. He was looking at her searchingly. He was obviously coming to the point at last.

"Ten thousand pounds," he said, "would cover the whole thing."

"Ten thousand pounds!" she screamed. "I haven't got it."

"Of course not," he said soothingly, "but any small contribution . . ." He rose. "Perhaps you'd like time to think it over?"

"Yes, I should," said Miss Gaye hysterically.

"There is no hurry, of course," he said. "I'll call again. Don't trouble to see me out."

She heard the sound of the starting up of the ramshackle car, then the scream of his brakes as he narrowly avoided a couple of hens that had strayed into the road.

She sat back in her chair, intending to abandon herself to the relief of hysterics . . . when the door opened and a small tense-looking woman, dressed in a knitted suit and a straw hat of the sort that was known as "mushroom" in the far-off days of its vogue, entered the room.

"Forgive me for coming in like this," she said, "but the door was ajar and I'm a great friend of Miss Featherstone's, so I'm afraid I just did it without thinking."

"Oh, yes . . . Miss Featherstone," said Gloria vaguely, putting off the hysterics to a more convenient moment and turning her thoughts to the precise, elderly spinster from whom she had rented the cottage. "Yes . . . Miss Featherstone. I remember her."

"Of course you do," said the visitor rather tartly. "My name's Miss Abbot, by the way, and I've come to see if my cat's here."

"Your cat?" said Miss Gaye, clinging with all her might to her sanity and self-control. "Why should your cat be here?"

"He wanders and"—fixing a bright accusing eye on her hostess—"I hear that he's been seen in the immediate vicinity of this cottage. Alice Featherstone made rather a pet of him, so I naturally took for granted that——"

"No," said Miss Gaye stonily, "I haven't seen him."

"You're sure?" said Miss Abbot. "*Quite* sure?"

"Quite sure," said Miss Gaye.

"He's a very handsome tom, and I can quite understand anyone wanting to keep him as a pet."

"I don't want to keep him as a pet," said Miss Gaye.

"It's rather odd that he isn't here," said Miss Abbot. "He was seen so near and so recently. And, as I say, he so often came to see Miss Featherstone."

"I haven't got your cat," said Miss Gaye slowly and distinctly.

"You'll let me know at once, I hope, if he comes here?"

"Yes."

Miss Abbot's keen eyes were darting about the room.

"Do you mind?" she said, going to a small reading-lamp and moving it from the bureau to a little table. "Miss Featherstone always had it there." Her eyes darted round again, and she took up a saucer containing some cigarette-ends from the bookcase, examining it with tightened lips. "I don't think that Miss Featherstone would care to see this saucer used as an ash-tray."

"It was on the chimney-piece," said Miss Gaye in self-defence.

"I know. It was there as an ornament. This saucer is part of a tea-set that belonged to Miss Featherstone's grandmother—the only surviving part, as it happens—and has very dear associations for her. Perhaps you'll have it washed and replaced on the chimney-piece?"

Miss Gaye muttered something.

"Well, I'll be going now," said Miss Abbot, making her way into the hall. "Don't trouble to see me out. I know my way in this house. . . . And you'll send me word at once if my Tom turns up, won't you?"

Miss Gaye made no answer. She was sitting on the settee, drawing a long deep breath.

"Miss *Gaye!*" called Miss Abbot sharply from the hall.

Gloria stopped in the middle of her breath, got up and went into the hall. Miss Abbot stood, her mouth pursed with horror, holding a paper bag that she had just taken up from the small oak chest. It contained a pound of grapes that Gloria had bought in Hadley that morning. A certain number were evidently over-ripe, and one corner of the bag was sodden with moisture. There was a damp patch on the chest from which Miss Abbot had just removed it.

"Look at this!" said Miss Abbot, her mouth so tightly pursed that she seemed to speak with difficulty. "*Look!*"

"What?" said Gloria innocently.

"That chest was left to Miss Featherstone by a very dear great-aunt. She would be more distressed than I can say."

"Why?" said Gloria, bewildered.

"I think you had better wipe it with a clean damp cloth, then give it a good polish."

"Oh, that!" said Gloria, realising at last what Miss Abbot meant.

"Yes," said Miss Abbot. "I shouldn't like Miss Featherstone to come home and find *that* sort of thing."

She whisked into the kitchen with the grapes, then, coming back into the hall, ran her finger along the top of a small framed sampler and held it out to Gloria.

"Look!" she said. "*Filthy!*"

"Well, you can wash," said Gloria, misunderstanding the cause of her distress, "and you needn't have done it."

"It can't have been dusted for *days*."

"There's a woman to do the work," said Gloria. "A Mrs. Bump or Jump or something."

"Mump," said Miss Abbot, "Fanny Mump. Don't you supervise her?"

"No," said Gloria.

"Fanny Mump," said Miss Abbot solemnly, "is no use at all unless she's supervised. Anyone in the village could have told you that. Miss Featherstone supervises everything she does." She bent down and lifted up a corner of the rug that covered the hall floor. "*There!*" she said dramatically. "She's not had the rug up since Miss Featherstone went away. You must make her take it up and put it on the lawn and give the whole floor a good clean and polish. It's the only way, Miss Gaye. You must go round after her and *see* that she does her work. Otherwise, the whole place will go to rack and ruin."

"It can, for all I care," muttered Gloria.

"I beg your pardon, Miss Gaye?" said Miss Abbot icily. "What did you say?"

"Nothing." said Gloria sulkily.

"Don't think I'm blaming you, Miss Gaye," said Miss Abbot more kindly. "In films, of course, there is no need for order or method, but a *house*," reverently, "is different. Well, I won't keep you any longer. You'll let me know about my cat at once if he comes here, won't you? Good-bye."

She went to the door, darted back and moved the umbrella stand a few inches nearer the hat-stand, went to the door again, darted back and put a pair of gloves, that Miss Petworth had left on the hat-stand, into the hat-stand drawer, then returned to the door and looked up and down the road.

"Here's my niece," she said. "She's kindly helping me in my search for my cat. Well, good-bye."

She went down to the gate and scurried off in the direction of the village.

Gloria meant to return at once to the settee and the interrupted attack of hysterics, but something about the approaching figure interested her, and she stayed at the door, watching it. Most people here went about in old faded cotton frocks or shabby tweeds, but this figure didn't. It tottered on a pair of three-inch heels, it wore nylons and a full gathered skirt of black satin with a black chiffon blouse, and it had a hat composed of black and white flowers with an eye veil. It wore gloves and ear-rings and was heavily made up. Moreover, it was, Miss Gaye saw as it came nearer, extremely pretty.

Having satisfied her curiosity, she was about to turn back, when she saw that the figure was opening the gate. . . .

* * *

Rosalyn had not gone straight to Honeysuckle Cottage after her interview with William. She had set out immediately, it is true, but had realised suddenly that she wore her oldest frock, that her hair was a sight and that she was only half made-up. She was, she decided, in no state to join issues with a film star. So she returned home and spent a good hour in preparation for the combat. She gave deep and earnest thought to the black shirt and blouse. She wasn't quite sure that it was suitable for the weather or place or time of day, but it was undeniably smart, and it imparted to her a widow-like look that fitted in well with the circumstances. She re-did her hair six times, and re-made-up her face seven. The shoes she had bought from a friend and had never dared to wear till now, but she found that if she walked carefully she could manage quite well, though they were, she discovered after she'd worn them for a few minutes, a little on the small side. While she was dressing, her aunt had rung up and asked her to help look for Tom, who had vanished again, and Rosalyn had answered absently that she would, her mind all the time exercised by the problem as to whether to wear her pearl ear-rings or her paste ones. She decided on the paste ones. They had, she thought, a *married* look, which contributed to the general widow-like effect. . . . As she put them on, dabbing behind her ears a generous allowance of the perfume that Robert had given her on her birthday last month, she rehearsed the scene to herself, trying various methods of approach, practising pathos, anger, scorn, pleading, renunciation, in turn before her looking-glass. She crossed renunciation off her list after one trial, deciding that it wasn't in her line.

Even now, as she walked, with a certain amount of difficulty, towards Honeysuckle Cottage, she hadn't quite made up her mind on the exact method she would use. She had resolved not to waste any time on preliminaries. She would leap at once into the heart of the scene. But she still hadn't chosen her opening lines. She'd tried: "Give him back to me, Miss Gaye," and "Do you want to kill me, Miss Gaye?" and "What is he to you, Miss Gaye?" and she liked them all. She would probably use them all, and leave to fate the decision as to which should come first.

Her courage began to fail as she approached the cottage, and it is possible that, if she had not seen Gloria Gaye standing in the open doorway, she might have gone past it. But the sight of Gloria Gaye was a challenge that she could not refuse.

She opened the small gate and walked up to the front door.

"Are you Miss Gaye?" she said, deciding that the woman was well over thirty.

"Yes," said Gloria, deciding that the girl had on the wrong shade of lipstick, the wrong shade of rouge, the wrong perfume and the wrong size in shoes, and that the whole outfit was wrong for wandering about country lanes, looking for cats. "Come in."

"I'm Rosalyn Abbot," said Rosalyn.

"Oh, yes . . ." said Gloria. "Her niece. She told me about you."

Rosalyn wasn't listening. She was making a swift choice of her opening lines. She faced Gloria across the little sitting-room, head thrown back proudly, eyes flashing. "Miss Gaye," she said, "give him back to me."

Gloria sighed. She was sick to death of that cat.

"I haven't got him," she said wearily.

"You have. You've stolen him from me."

"I have not," said Gloria. "You can search the house if you don't believe me."

"I'm not implying," said Rosalyn, with curling lip, "that you've actually got him concealed on the premises."

"What are you implying then?"

"You know quite well what I'm implying. You don't *want* him, do you?"

"No," said Gloria.

"Then why have you stolen him from me? What can he mean to a woman like you? To me he means *everything*. You take him just for a few days' pleasure, but to me——" She tried to put a sob into her voice, but realised that it didn't quite come off and cleared her throat instead. "Miss Gaye, won't you give him back to me?"

"Now, listen, Miss Abbot," said Gloria with rising anger, "I've told you once and I tell you again, I haven't got him, I don't want him and I'm not interested in tom cats."

"How *dare* you!" said Rosalyn and, turning on her heels (she managed it quite well), swept from the cottage without another word.

Miss Gaye sat down on the settee. She thought of hysterics but realised that the mood had passed.

"Kay!" she called.

Miss Petworth came downstairs, twirling her spectacles.

"You've had quite a lot of visitors," she said. "Anyone interesting?"

"We're going back to London to-morrow, Kay," said Gloria in a voice choked by emotion.

"What about the rest cure?" said Miss Petworth.

"Rest cure?" said Gloria, laughing wildly. "I've been bullied, insulted, blackmailed and accused of stealing cats all in one afternoon. If this is a rest cure, give me Euston Station. We're going back to London first thing to-morrow."

"O.K. by me," said Miss Petworth.

Chapter 12

William approached the old barn slowly and despondently, with Jumble at his heels.

The three other Outlaws were awaiting him, and
he could see by their expressions that they had fared
no better than himself in their quest for their entrance
money to the profession of tramp. Douglas carried a
paper bag. The rest had their hands thrust into their
pockets and stood in attitudes of dejection.

"Any good?" they asked him.

"No," said William. "They've not got any *sense*,
haven't my family. I offered to save 'em hundreds of
pounds jus' for two shillings an' they wouldn't even
listen. They say I don't know the value of money,
but it's them that doesn't. . . . No wonder," bitterly,
"my father's not a rich man, throwin' away hundreds
of pounds in one afternoon. What about you?"

"I did my best, too," said Ginger. "I offered to let
'em knock off whatever they were goin' to give me for
Christmas, an' they wouldn't even let me go on talkin'
about it. Started on about all I cost 'em for food an'
school bills."

"So did mine," said Douglas. "Well, we can't
help eatin' food, can we? We've gotter *live*, haven't
we, same as them? An' it's jolly rotten food, some of
it, too."

"An' we don't want to go to school," said Henry. "It's them that makes us."

"I offered to give up school," said Douglas. "I said I'd teach myself out of books, if they'd give me jus' two shillings. That'd have saved them pounds an' pounds. Well, that's all schoolmasters do. They jus' learn things out of books an' then teach them us. It'd save a lot of money an' time if we jus' got the books an' learnt 'em ourselves. An' then there wouldn't be any schoolmasters an' a jolly good thing, too."

"P'raps they think we wouldn't learn 'em," said Henry, who was more of a realist than the other three.

"Well, why should we?" said William. "Savages don't, an' savages are jolly fine people. I bet I'd sooner have a savage for a father than mine. Goin' on an' on about first one thing an' then another. I bet a savage can use his garter for a catapult without all that fuss."

"They don't have 'em," said Henry.

"Oh, well, never mind," said William, tiring of the subject. "Didn't you get anythin'?"

"No," said Henry. "I said I'd have somethin' else taken out of me for two shillings, an' it'd be *cheap*, 'cause they gave me five shillings for havin' my appendix out, but they wouldn't take any notice. Went on an' on about a few ole flowers I'd—I'd borrowed for Ethel. I say"—to William—"you couldn't get 'em back, could you? It might stop 'em goin' on an' on about 'em if I got 'em back."

"I'll try," said William. "Depends on where she's put 'em."

"It's *stealin'* for her to keep 'em," said Henry.

"Couldn't you appeal to her sense of honour, same as ole Markie does to us at school?"

"She hasn't got one," said William bitterly. "None of my family has," adding as an afterthought, " 'cept me."

"All right," said Henry gloomily. "I s'pose they'll go on an' on an' on about those flowers till I'm an ole man."

"Be all right if a few more people wanted a few shilling wrongs righted."

"I *said* a shilling was too much," said Douglas. "There *isn't* anyone with more than fourpence—not that I know, anyway. No one's even left a note."

"Well, someone might still. The notice is still up."

But it wasn't. As they turned their heads to look at it, a breeze detached it from its precarious fastening, and it floated down to the ground. Immediately, Jumble leapt upon it and tore it to shreds. Jumble had paper-tearing moods, when not even Mr. Brown's *Times* was sacred to him, and he was evidently working up for one now.

"Oh, well," said William resignedly. "It didn't seem to do much good."

Douglas was opening his paper bag. "Look!" he said. "We had some people to tea an' I bagged the sandwich crusts. There's a jolly lot of fish paste on some of 'em."

Their spirits rose, and they sat down in a circle on the grass just outside the barn door, while Douglas emptied out his treasure trove. Jumble joined the circle, looking hopefully at the sandwich crusts and thumping his tail on the ground. They were, on the whole, an encouraging sight. A few were, of course, merely dry bread, but on most of them largish clumps of marge and bits of fish paste made a good showing.

"Let's divide 'em," said William, "and choose in turns."

For the next few minutes their whole attention was given to the division of the sandwich crusts, each making his choice with frowning concentration, weighing up the advantages of so much fish paste against so much marge, of a smaller portion of marge and paste mixed, against a larger portion of marge or fish paste alone. Such crusts as contained neither were put in a little pile in front of Jumble.

"She's jolly good at sandwich crusts," said Douglas, referring to his family's maid. "She spreads right to the end and cuts a lot off. My mother's rotten. She just spreads the middle and cuts hardly any off."

"Mine's like that, too," said Henry.

They munched happily and in silence for some moments, during which a considerable lightening of the atmosphere took place.

"After all," said William, "we righted *one* wrong all right. We found a home for Mr. Rose."

"A jolly good one, too."

"I bet we only went wrong tryin' to get 'em married, 'cause we tried too many at once, an' it got us into a sort of muddle. If we'd tried only one . . ."

"Hi! Jumble's pinched my best piece."

"Give it back, Jumble."

Ginger, being troubled by no hygienic scruples, ate with relish the crust that William retrieved from Jumble's mouth.

"Well, let's try only one."

"Let's try Robert."

"It's houses that's the trouble. People won't get married till they've got a house."

"Well, we've found one for Mr. Rose."

"Y-yes, but that's diff'rent. We've jus' found a place for him to rest in when he's tired. He won't be livin' there all the time same as Robert an' Gloria Gaye would want to. Mrs. Bott wouldn't have Robert an' Gloria Gaye livin' there all the time, an' I bet Robert wouldn't want to, 'cause he doesn't like Mrs. Bott."

"Well, I don't see how we can get him a proper house. They're all lived in by people already."

"People go out of houses sometimes, don't they? There wouldn't be any removin' vans if they didn't, an' you see lots of removin' vans on the roads."

"Why do they go out of houses?"

"They die, sometimes."

William considered this. "I don't think we ought axshully to kill anyone," he said, as if abandoning the idea with reluctance.

"I heard of someone once that left a house 'cause the roof leaked."

"An' my aunt knew someone once that left a house 'cause it was haunted."

A tense look came over William's face. There was a thoughtful frown on his brow and a faraway expression in his eyes.

They watched him in respectful silence, knowing that one of his ideas was slowly forming in his mind.

"*Tell* you what!" he said at last.

"Yes?" they said eagerly.

"We've gotter find a house an' turn the people out, so's Robert an' Gloria Gaye can get married an' live in it."

"What house?"

"Well," said William, reflectively, putting his last

crust into his mouth, "we'd better not try to get rid of people that's been here a long time, like Miss Milton an' Gen'ral Moult, 'cause it'd take too long. They wouldn't want to go. An' other people'd come along tryin' to help them and mend the roof an' that sort of thing. We've got to choose people that haven't been here long an' that other people wouldn't want to help."

"I know!" said Ginger. "Ole Monkey Face."

"*Yes!*" said William. "That's a jolly good idea. An' he turned us off the tadpole pond an' he was rude to my mother in the post office, so it'll jolly well serve him right."

"But how'll we get rid of him?"

"We'll make the roof leak."

"How can we?"

"Well, a roof leakin' means water comin' through the roof, doesn't it? Well, you can make water come through a roof, can't you? You only need a bucket of water. There's nearly always a skylight or somethin'."

They were silent, aware that William's plan, as usual, was going to involve them in a series of complicated adventures and probably bring retribution in its train. But it never occurred to them to withdraw from it. Adventures with William were generally worth the trouble—trouble that on previous occasions had proved to be not inconsiderable.

"S'pose he doesn't go?" said Henry.

"We'll make him go," said William. "We'll haunt him as well."

"How?"

"Oh, jus' haunt him," said William carelessly. "Moanin' and groanin' and movin' things about."

"But we can't go inside his house," said Douglas.

"Why not?" said William. The Idea was taking hold of him and assuming larger proportions every second. "Why couldn't we? I bet there's not many houses I can't get inside when I try. An' I'd like to scare old Monkey Face away. 'Sides——"

"Yes?"

"If we found Robert a house, I bet he'd give us each two shillings for that tramp thing."

"Do you think he would?"

Their interest in the plan was growing.

"I 'spect he would," said Henry. "Proper agents make people pay a good deal more than that. They call it a premium. I've heard grown-ups talkin' about it."

"All right," said Ginger simply. "When do we start?"

"To-night," said William. "But we've got to go an' have a good look at the house first. You can't haunt a house till you know where everythin' is."

"Seems—seems sort of dangerous to me," said Douglas nervously.

" 'Course it's dangerous," said William. "You've got to go through a bit of danger for a bike an' two shillings. It's jolly well worth it."

The others agreed that it was.

"Well, we know what it's like inside," said Douglas. "We've been to tea when Miss Maurice was there. There's suits of armour an' things."

"She let us get into them once, d'you remember?" said Ginger, "an' we found we could move about in 'em. She let us play joustin' in 'em. She was jolly decent."

"I fell over in mine," said Douglas.

"I don't see why we shouldn't use 'em for the hauntin'," said William. "Suits of armour movin' about! It'd be jolly creepy."

"You've gotter have a real ghost for hauntin'," said Ginger.

"All right," said William. "We could manage that, too. We could take our sheets an' wrap them round us an'—an'—an' *flit* about in 'em same as in a ghost story."

The idea was taking shape and form in their minds as a reality. Their spirits rose exultantly.

"What about moanin' an' groanin'?" asked Ginger.

"That's easy enough," said William. "We'd have to practise a bit first, of course."

"Couldn't we rattle chains?" said Douglas.

"No, we haven't got any chains to rattle," said William. "I know where there's an ole watch-chain that used to belong to my grandfather, but it wouldn't make the sort of rattle anyone'd hear."

"I could get the rattle that my brother had on V-Day," said Ginger.

"In all the pictures of ghosts I've seen," said Henry, "they carried their heads under their arms."

"Don't be silly," said William. "We couldn't poss'bly do that. There's no sense in it either. Why did they, anyway?"

"I don't know. It was jus' a picture. It was s'posed to be a picture of a *real* one, though."

"All the pictures of real ones I've seen," said Douglas, "were jus' white."

"Gosh! It'd be fun to be a *real* one," said William. "Goin' about scarin' people every night."

"I bet it wouldn't be much fun," said Henry. "You couldn't eat ice-cream or sweets or choc'late biscuits or anythin'. They'd drop straight through you on to the ground."

"You could pick 'em up."

"You couldn't. Your fingers go through them."

"Then how could you put 'em in your mouth to start with for them to drop through?"

"Oh, shut up," said William. "Let's go on with fixin' up this hauntin'. We'll take sheets an' we'll get into the suits of armour an' we'll have a bucket of water to pour through somethin' an'——"

"I once read a story about a haunted house," said Ginger, "where the lights kept goin' off and on."

"We couldn't do that," said Douglas.

"Yes, we could," said William excitedly. "Don't you remember when we went down into that cellar with Miss Maurice an' she showed us where the main switch was? Well, we could turn all the switches in all the rooms on, an' then one of us could be in the cellar turnin' the main switch on and off, an' that'd make all the lights in all the rooms go on an' off."

"Gosh, yes! But how'd we get into the cellar?"

"Well, part of it's a coal cellar an' I think there's a sort of hole outside for tippin' the coal into it. We'll have to go an' explore first."

"Y-yes," said Douglas, "but we ought to make quite sure no one's in. I still think it's goin' to be dangerous."

"They'll have to be in when we haunt them. It's not much use haunting a house if there's no one in it."

"No," said William, "but we'll wait till midnight when they're asleep to do that. Then we'll wake 'em with moanin' and groanin'."

"Midnight?" said Douglas. "But we'll be in bed."

"Well, we can get up, can't we?" said William, and added, with the guffaw that was his usual tribute to his own wit, " 'less we're sleepin' in cement, of course, and it's news to *me* we sleep in cement."

"What do we do first?" said Henry.

"We'll go to the Manor now," said William, "an', if ole Monkey Face an' Toad Face are out of the way, we'll jus' have a look round an' see if that coal thing's all right. Come on. An' we'll go past the Hall in the ditch 'case Violet Elizabeth's anywhere about. We jolly well aren't havin' her in *this*. I'll take Jumble home first, too. He'd only mess up hauntin'."

"Dogs' hairs stand on end when they meet ghosts."

"Well, Jumble's wouldn't, if we were the ghosts. He'd start tryin' to play with us an' knock somethin' over."

William left Jumble at home, hurrying out of the house before his mother could ask him where he was going and pretending not to hear when the question was thrown after him down the garden path.

In single file they crept past the Hall in the ditch, successfully evading any watch that Violet Elizabeth might have been keeping for them.

Slowly, rather apprehensively, they approached the gate of the Manor. The drive was empty. The house looked empty.

"I bet he's out," said William. "Come on, let's go in."

They went up the drive to the house, keeping well in the shelter of the trees, Douglas showing a tendency to stay behind every few yards to tie up his shoe lace.

The house still seemed empty. They walked round to the back.

"Yes, look!" said William. "Here it is! It's got a little ring an' you pull it out an' then you get down into the coal cellar. An' from that you get to the other cellar where the main light switches are an'——"

A growl interrupted him, and a heavy hand descended on his neck. Looking up, his eyes met the small fierce eyes of the man in the check sports coat. The man's other hand had secured Ginger, while Henry and Douglas were making their way down the drive as fast as they could.

"Next time I find any of you kids here," he said in a low savage voice, "I'll cut your livers out. See? I'll cut your livers out and skin you alive."

With that he cracked their heads together, then flung them on to the ground, aiming an ineffectual kick at them as they rolled away.

"D'you want any more?" he said, raising his voice and hand threateningly.

They didn't. They scrambled to their feet and ran as best they could down to the gate, where Douglas and Henry were waiting for them.

"Gosh! he nearly killed you," said Henry.

"I said it was dangerous," said Douglas in gloomy triumph. "I shouldn't be surprised if it ends in death."

"Well, we'll jolly well haunt him now, all right," said William, rubbing his head. "He's asked for it now."

They walked down the road for some yards, then looked back.

The man in the check sports coat had come down to the gate.

"And I'll put the police on to you, too, you young devils," he shouted.

They hastened their footsteps. Suddenly Hubert Lane's head appeared over the hedge.

He had evidently been crossing the field and had seen and heard most of what had happened.

"Thought you worked with the p'lice, William

A HEAVY HAND DESCENDED ON WILLIAM. LOOKING
UP, HIS EYES MET THOSE OF THE MAN IN THE CHECK
SPORTS COAT, WHOSE OTHER HAND HAD SECURED
GINGER.

Brown," he said mockingly. "Thought you were in with them."

William was taken aback for a moment but quickly recovered himself.

"Have you never heard of people workin' with the p'lice an' pretendin' not to, so's to lead crim'nals on?" he said. "Well, that's what I do. That's what I do for the p'lice, an' they're jolly grateful to me, too."

Hubert gave a jeering laugh, then, at a threatening movement from William, set off at a run across the field.

Henry was gazing through the hedge that skirted the grounds of the Manor.

"Can you see Monkey Face?" said William.

"Yes. . . . He's jus' goin' in at the front door."

* * *

The man in the check sports coat entered the hall and closed the front door behind him.

The man he had called Boss came out of the room on the right that had been Miss Maurice's drawing-room. He still wore his chauffeur's uniform.

"What was it, Tonks?" he said.

"Those kids from the village," said the other. "The ones that are always trying to get at the pond."

"I thought I'd told you to keep them out."

"I don't think they'll come again. I gave them something to remember."

"And I told you I didn't want scenes. The less notice this place gets the better."

"O.K., Boss."

Tonks stood gazing round the hall. Very little light came through the stained-glass window. The suits of armour on the stairs had a vaguely sinister look in the general gloom.

He shivered.

"I get the willies all the time I'm in this place," he said. "Shouldn't be surprised to meet a ghost here any bloomin' night after dark. No kiddin'."

"Well," said the Boss, "if you meet anyone prowling about after dark, hit him first and find out if he's a ghost afterwards."

Tonks gave a start and looked fearfully over his shoulder, as the branch of a tree moved in the breeze just across the window.

"It gives me the willies, good and proper," he said. "I shall be glad when we can pack up."

The Boss crossed the hall and, going to a cocktail cabinet by the fireplace, poured out two glasses of whisky.

"Here's a willie-chaser," he said, handing one to Tonks. "But don't have too many of them. You've got to be on your toes to-night." He took out his watch. "I must be off now."

"I'll be all right," said Tonks nervously. "I sleep with all the lights on."

"You won't to-night."

"Say, Boss," pleaded Tonks, "I can't sleep in the dark. No kiddin'—I can't."

"You'll have to. Can't have all the lights blazing here to-night."

"Then I won't go to bed at all."

"You'll go to bed as soon as the deliveries are here," said the Boss shortly. "There's not much sleep for any of us for the next forty-eight hours, so get what you can. I'll come in with the pick-up convoy at twelve-thirty. Set an alarm for that time and get up as soon as you hear it. Don't use the phone. They keep records."

He moved towards the front door. Tonks followed him, his wizened face long with misery.

"Men have got the George Cross for less than sleeping here with the lights out, Boss—no kiddin'."

"You'll get ten years if you botch to-night. An' that's no kiddin' neither." He opened the front door. "Don't come out with me. I've got the car in the drive all ready. . . . And no more willie-chasers, remember."

He vanished, slamming the front door behind him.

Tonks stood there, listening to the sound of the car dying away in the distance.

Then he turned back into the hall and stood motionless, looking around nervously. . . . Suddenly an expression of terror contorted his features.

Somewhere in the distance rose an eerie sound, gathering volume, dying away . . . gathering volume . . . dying away.

Tonks shivered.

"Owls," he said, reassuring himself and making his way over to the cabinet.

But it wasn't.

It was the Outlaws practising their moans.

Chapter 13

Robert Brown and Richard Merridew were waiting in the lounge of the Grand Hotel, Hadley. They were waiting for Rosalyn Abbot and Valerie Greyston respectively. Both had booked tables for dinner early in the week and were looking forward to an evening of innocent dalliance. The two boys had known each other from childhood, had attended the same school and were on friendly terms. They were chatting together amicably now, discussing local events and the chances of the village cricket team in various forthcoming matches.

But they kept a wary eye on the door. . . .

Rosalyn and Valerie, too, had attended the same school and until a fortnight ago had been bosom friends. But a fortnight ago an ill-advised comment, made by Valerie on a new hat of Rosalyn's and repeated to Rosalyn by a mutual friend, had caused a breach in the friendship. They met each other now in the village without sign of recognition. They stood side by side in the queue in Hadley's most select chemist's on the Elizabeth Arden quota day, each gazing abstractedly into the distance.

Robert and Richard accommodated themselves to this situation with the elasticity of youth. When alone together, they talked easily and naturally. When in company with the beloveds, they ignored each other with a blankness that satisfied even the beloveds.

Suddenly Robert saw Rosalyn approaching the door and, breaking off short in the middle of a few simple aspersions that he was casting on the integrity of the umpire of Upper Marleigh Second Cricket eleven, he went over to the wall, where he stood absorbed apparently in an engraving of Landseer's Monarch of the Glen.

Richard, grasping the situation, went over to the other wall and studied an enlarged photograph of the Victoria Falls.

Rosalyn entered. It appeared to be a few seconds before Robert realised her presence. Then he turned round with a start of surprise and delight.

"Oh, there you are!" he said.

"Yes, here I am," said Rosalyn.

He realised at once that something was wrong and searched frantically in his mind for the reason. He hadn't kept her waiting. He'd changed into his best suit (she'd made a scene once because he'd turned up in flannels and a sports coat). He'd rung her up in the morning to remind her of the appointment (once she had forgotten to come and had said that she couldn't possibly be expected to remember every trivial engagement throughout a whole week), with appropriate expressions of affection and pleasurable anticipation. . . . It couldn't be any of those.

Suddenly it occurred to him that perhaps (she had very good eyesight) she had seen him fraternising with Richard. Fraternising with Richard was, in her eyes, "taking Valerie's part against her". . . . Oh well, she'd soon get over it.

They entered the restaurant, and the head-waiter

showed them to a small table against the wall.

Almost immediately afterwards he showed Richard and Valerie to another small table next to them. It was an awkward situation, but the two couples met it by continuing to ignore each other. Robert, however, wasn't so much taken up by his own troubles that he didn't notice that Valerie, too, was upset about something. Perhaps she, too, had seen the fraternisation that in her eyes was "taking Rosalyn's part against her". Oh, well, they'd both soon get over it. He began to chat in a pleasant, casual fashion to Rosalyn, trying to charm away her sulkiness. He'd done it before, times innumerable. At a certain point in the conversation, the dimples would peep out in her cheeks, and all would be well. But though he worked like a cart-horse (as he put it to himself), the point seemed as far off as ever. Both Rosalyn's manner and the dimples remained distant.

Listening at intervals to the conversation at the next table, he realised with a certain satisfaction that Richard, trying the same tactics, was getting no better results. At last he took the bull by the horns.

"Is anything the matter, dear?" he said.

Rosalyn raised reproachful eyes from her sausage meat *à la milanaise*.

"How can you ask?" she said with a gulp of emotion.

"But I can," said Robert. "I mean, I do. I am doing."

"You *know* what's the matter," said Rosalyn in broken accents. "You *know*——"

"I——" began Robert, but, catching the words, "rotten pineapple" spoken by Valerie in soul-stirring tones at the next table, stopped to listen. Rosalyn, too, let her attention wander.

Richard, like Robert, had decided to take the bull by the horns.

"I know we had a bit of a tiff on Wednesday, Val," he said pleadingly, "but I said I was sorry. I proved I was sorry . . ."

"It was a nice proof, wasn't it?" said Valerie hysterically. "A rotten pineapple!"

"What d'you mean, a rotten pineapple?" said the bewildered Richard.

"Oh, don't deny it! I got the message and everything. I suppose you thought it was funny. I——"

Robert and Rosalyn turned back to their own scene.

"What do I know?" said Robert.

"You know what you've done to me. If you love her better than me, *go* to her, that's all."

"Love who?"

"Gloria Gaye."

"Gloria Gaye?"

He stared at her, stupefied, and they remained silent while the waiter removed their plates and brought them the dried apricots and still more dried shreds of apple that figured as "fruit salad" on the menu.

"Did you say Gloria Gaye?" repeated Robert when he had gone.

"Yes, and you needn't think she loves you, because she doesn't. She *told* me she didn't. She called you a tom cat."

"Who did?" said Robert, so confused that he hardly knew what they were talking about.

"Gloria Gaye."

"Called me what?"

"A tom cat."

"Why?"

"I suppose she thinks you're like one."

At the mention of Gloria Gaye, the couple at

the next table had stopped talking and were listening
intently.

"Look here!" said Robert slowly. "Are you accusing
me of carrying on with Gloria Gaye?"

"Doesn't your own conscience accuse you?"

"No, it doesn't," said Robert stoutly.

"I have proof," said Rosalyn.

"What proof?"

"Sending presents to a woman like that and"—with
a vague idea of making the crime seem more
heinous—"through an innocent child!"

"What innocent child?"

"William," said Rosalyn, rather lamely.

Robert gave a harsh laugh.

"It's the first time I've ever heard him called that."

"That's right," flared Rosalyn. "Run down your
own family now you've broken my heart."

Richard and Valerie turned back to take up the
threads of their own scene, but a little half-heartedly,
afraid of missing something good at the next table.

"I've never been so insulted in my life," said
Valerie. "A rotten pineapple!"

"*What* rotten pineapple?" said Richard. "I don't
even know what you're talking about."

"You can't deny that you sent me a rotten
pineapple by"—she was tempted to use the "innocent
child" theme, but decided that she wouldn't use Rosalyn
Abbot's leavings even in an argument—"by—by a third
person," she ended.

"I did *not*," said Richard.

She waved his denial aside.

"It couldn't even have been a joke. It was a
deliberate insult. It wasn't only rotten. It looked
as if it had been kicked about the road. That *you*

should do a thing like that to me, Richard. It's—well, it's fantastic."

Then she turned an ear to the next table.

"I am *not* carrying on with Gloria Gaye," Robert was saying.

"Why did you send her flowers, then?"

"I didn't send her flowers."

"You did. Don't prevaricate."

"I'm not prevaricating. I don't believe you even know what the word means."

"I do. It means telling lies."

"Well, it doesn't. It means speaking evasively."

"That's right. Try to change the subject."

"I'm not changing the subject. You used the word, and I thought you might as well know what it meant, in case you ever want to use it again."

"Anything, of course, to stop me getting at the truth about Gloria Gaye!"

The waiter brought the coffee.

Valerie returned to her own scene.

"When I think of all the things you said to me that Sunday when we were on the river—what a difference I'd made in your whole life and that sort of thing—and to think it ends in this, you sending me a rotten pineapple."

"Why on earth should I send you a rotten pineapple?" said Richard.

"That *is* prevaricating," said Valerie a little uncertainly.

"I suppose you've been at the cottage this evening. To come straight to me—*me*, from a woman like that!"

"I've never set foot in her cottage."

"Whichever way you look at it, a rotten pineapple's an insult."

"I never sent it to you."

"Prove that you didn't, then."

"How can I?"

"I know you have your faults, Robert, but I didn't know you were a philanderer. I didn't know that you'd come straight from a woman like that to me."

"I took it to mean and I still take it to mean that everything is over between us. A rotten pineapple couldn't mean anything else."

"And how many more film stars have you got in cottages all over the country? How long have you been deceiving me?"

"You didn't even try to hide what you meant. The more I think of it the more I realise what a brute you are and what a good thing it is I've found out in time."

And then simultaneously, each word exactly synchronising, the two girls said:

"I never want to see or speak to you again."

They turned and looked at each other, conquering a strong inclination to put out their hands, cross fingers, wish and say "Shakespeare."

Robert and Richard, too, turned and looked at each other, and an electric spark seemed to pass between them. In silence their eyes flashed a question and an answer. In silence they rose, went to the head-waiter, settled their accounts, and walked out of the hotel.

They walked in silence for some yards down the street. Then Richard said:

"They shouldn't have said it if they didn't mean it."

"Exactly," said Robert.

"I felt I couldn't stand another minute of it."

"So did I. What was the trouble?"

"I don't know. Something about a pineappple. I couldn't make head or tail of it. I hate the things, anyway, except tinned. What was yours?"

"I don't know. Something about Gloria Gaye."

"Well, it ought to be a lesson to them."

"Exactly."

They spoke without conviction, both secretly aware of the long weeks of grovelling penitence and expensive entertainment by which they would have to pay for their gesture of manly pride and independence.

"I've put up with a lot from her one way and another."

"So have I."

"She *can* be very sweet, of course."

"So can Rosalyn."

They walked in silence for a few more yards, then Richard said:

"I wonder what they're doing now?"

"Perhaps they're just sitting there."

"Perhaps they've gone home."

"Perhaps they're tearing each other's eyes out."

*   *   *

They were doing none of these things. Valerie had taken Robert's seat, and the two were deep in confidential converse, all their differences forgotten.

"The childishness of men!" Valerie was saying. "The utter childishness!"

"Incredible, isn't it?" said Rosalyn.

"Fantastic," agreed Valerie.

"Really it's quite a relief to be without them. They get on one's nerves so horribly sometimes, don't they?"

"Unspeakably," agreed Valerie.

"What was it?" said Rosalyn. "Something about a pineapple . . .?"

"Yes. He sent me one. He pretends now that he didn't, but he did. He must have done it in a moment of madness, but he did it. With a message, too."

"Rotten, I think you said."

"More than rotten."

"Perhaps it was all right when he sent it and went bad on the way. It's bad keeping weather, you know."

"If you'd seen it, you wouldn't have said that. It was fantastic. Has Robert——? I mean did he——?"

Rosalyn nodded.

"Gloria Gaye. He's been carrying on with her."

"Fancy!" said Valerie. "I didn't know he was that sort."

"He isn't, really," said Rosalyn. Shamelessly she borrowed Valerie's phrase. "He must have done it in a moment of madness, but he certainly did it. I know the person he sent flowers by."

"William, I think you said?"

"Well, yes," admitted Rosalyn.

"I heard that she'd taken Honeysuckle Cottage, but I haven't seen her yet. Have you?"

"Yes," said Rosalyn and gave a highly dramatised and wildly inaccurate account of her interview with Gloria.

"Gosh!" said Valerie, enthralled by the recital. "You absolutely wiped the floor with her."

"Yes, I did."

"You must have left her feeling an absolute worm."

"I think I did," said Rosalyn. "I think she'll leave Robert alone after this. . . . Of course," meditatively, "it shows that there's something *about* Robert, if a woman like that can fall for him."

"Is she pretty?"

"No. She's as near plain as you can be without actually *being* plain, if you know what I mean."

Valerie did. She nodded understandingly.

"Of course, they simply *carve* whole fresh faces on them at those film places to make them look pretty," she said. "It's fantastic."

"How Robert could have fallen for her!"

"Anyway, darling, it's lovely to have a nice chat with you again," said Valerie. "And I've been simply adoring your hat ever since you came in. Where did you get it?"

Chapter 14

As the last note of twelve sounded from the church clock, William got out of bed and put on his clothes. He had tried various devices for keeping himself awake . . . tying a piece of cotton on to his toe which he pulled at intervals till it broke . . . arranging round him in bed various scrubbing and carpet brushes and a fibre doormat, borrowed from the kitchen, so that when he moved in his sleep they would wake him . . . and putting under his pillow a pile of books that guaranteed an uncomfortable angle for his head.

Despite all this, he fell asleep at ten o'clock and awoke by sheer good luck on the last stroke of twelve.

When he had dressed, he took his sheet, bundled it under his arm and peeped out into the corridor. The coast was, as far as he could see, clear. The only disconcerting sign was a light under Robert's door.

Robert, after three telephone conversations with Rosalyn, in the last of which he seemed to be making a little—a very little—headway, had spent the last hour composing a letter to her, a letter that, he thought, should finally dispel the clouds of misunderstanding that seemed to have gathered about them, and, at a certain price (flowers, thank Heaven, were fairly cheap just now, and perhaps his father would lend him money to take her to a matinée or something in London), the affair might be restored to its old footing. The dictionary in which he had looked up the spelling of "impeachment" "equivocal" and "ecstasy" (his style inclined slightly to journalese and, though he was quite a good speller, he always liked to verify the longer words), lay open on the writing-table . . . He was so lost in roseate dreams of his final reconciliation with Rosalyn that even William's footsteps in the corridor outside would not have disturbed him. William, of course, could not know this. He tiptoed carefully and (almost) silently past the door. . . . He continued tiptoeing carefully and (almost) silently, looking back at that ominous line of light, prepared to make a bolt back to his own bedroom should the door suddenly fly open. Engrossed in this, he failed to notice the loft ladder that Mr. Brown had left leaning against the wall, after investigation of certain curious (but, as it turned out, harmless) noises that had issued from the cistern earlier in the evening.

The crash of the ladder falling heavily to the ground after its impact with William's solid frame re-echoed through the house. Without a moment's hesitation, William streaked back to his bedroom. Robert emerged first from his room, breaking off in the middle of a somewhat involved sentence that he didn't know how to finish, anyway.

Almost immediately Mr. Brown's bedroom door opened, and Mr. Brown, tousled and blinking, appeared in the doorway.

"What on earth was that?" he said.

Robert had switched on the light.

"Someone fell over the ladder," he said.

Mrs. Brown had now joined them.

"Do be careful, John," she said. "If it's a burglar you know how desperate they are nowadays. They shoot on sight."

Ethel's door opened.

"What is it?" she said.

"It's a burglar," explained Mrs. Brown. "He knocked over the ladder."

"I heard footsteps," said Mr. Brown. "I distinctly heard footsteps both before and after the crash. The best thing would be to search the house."

"*Take* something, dear," pleaded Mrs. Brown. "A poker or a revolver or something. Even William's air-gun would be better than nothing. It's on the wardrobe, you know. You took it from him for breaking the garden frame with it."

"I've still got that old service revolver," said Robert. "I'll take that."

Ethel had gone back to her room to take out her curlers, put on some make-up and change into her other dressing-gown. It was only a burglar, of course, but Ethel was the type of girl who likes to look her best even for a burglar.

When she emerged, Robert and Mr. Brown were just coming out of the spare bedroom.

"There's no one there," said Mr. Brown.

"Did you look under the bed?" said Mrs. Brown.

"Of course."

"And in the wardrobe?"

"Of course."

"You've searched the bathroom, haven't you?"

"We've looked into it. No one's there. You can't *search* a bathroom. A person's there or they aren't. Come on, Robert. We'll look in the downstairs rooms."

"You mustn't go without a weapon, John," said Mrs. Brown.

"Robert's got his revolver."

"He might miss him. You'll want something if it comes to a hand-to-hand struggle. Look." She took a brass stair rod out of the top stair. "Take this, John. John, I shan't let you go downstairs unless you take it."

Somewhat sheepishly, Mr. Brown allowed himself to be armed with a stair rod, and the two went downstairs.

Mrs. Brown and Ethel hung over the banisters, offering advice:

"Don't forget the coal cellar."

"Look in the hall cupboard."

"John, darling, don't carry that stair rod like a walking-stick. Have it *ready*."

"Are any windows open?"

"No."

"Has the front-door lock been tampered with?"

"No."

"Have you found anything, John?"

"Only a mouse in the mouse-trap."

"Good! That's the second this week."

The two came back upstairs.

"There's no one there," said Mr. Brown.

"Perhaps he's in the loft," suggested Ethel.

They stood, looking up at the trap-door.

"Why should he be?" said Mr. Brown.

"He might be hiding. That's probably what made the noise. He used the ladder to get up there and then let it drop."

"Why should he want to get up there?"

"Well, he might think we keep valuables up there. People do."

"JOHN, DON'T CARRY THAT STAIR ROD LIKE A WALKING
STICK," CALLED MRS. BROWN. "HAVE IT *READY*."

"What do you think, Robert?"

"Yes," said Robert vaguely. He'd just thought of a good ending for his sentence and was losing interest in the burglar. "Honestly, I don't think there's anyone here. Probably Dad put the ladder against the wall at a sort of angle and it fell. The force of gravity, you know."

"What do you think, Ethel?"

"I don't know," said Ethel rather pettishly. She was beginning to be afraid that there wasn't a burglar, after all. She'd never seen a burglar yet and had been looking forward to the experience.

"Well, now we've searched all the rest of the house," said Mr. Brown, who was becoming fired by the lust of the chase, "I don't think we ought to leave the loft. Will you go up or shall I, Robert?"

Then Emily's door opened. Emily was a notoriously heavy sleeper, but she had been roused at last. Her long face wore a grim reproachful look.

"I can't get a wink of sleep, mum," she said, "with all this 'ere talking going on. I've stood it as long as flesh an' blood can stand it."

"Didn't you hear a crash, Emily?"

"No," said Emily. "It's not my business hearin' crashes, an', if you like to talk out here all hours, it's not my place to complain, but if I can't get my night's rest I might as well give in my notice here and now. I'm sure I do my best and always 'ave done, but when it comes to the whole family talkin' all night on the landin', when they've got all day to talk downstairs—" she looked round the group and added, "All the family but one . . ."

"Yes," said Ethel slowly. "Where's William?"

There was a long, long silence, during which the

thoughts of all the Browns gradually converged at the same point. It was incredible that William should really be sleeping through the disturbance. It was equally incredible that William should not somehow be connected with any disturbance anywhere at any time.

As one man, they turned towards William's bedroom. William, foreseeing this as the inevitable end of the scene that was being enacted on the landing, had changed back into his pyjamas, swept his sleep-hindering devices under the bed, and was lying there with his eyes closed when they entered the room. They stood looking down at him. Aware of their scrutiny, he screwed up his eyes still more tightly, tried to snore, then cleared his throat in order to get a better effect.

"William!" said Mr. Brown.

William emitted an unconvincing snore.

"*William!*" bellowed Mr. Brown.

Not even William could pretend to sleep through that.

He opened his eyes and looked around with over-acted bewilderment.

"Where am I?" he said, playing for time.

"Have you been kicking ladders all over the house?" said Mr. Brown sternly.

"No, Father," said William, after giving the question a few moments' conscientious consideration.

"Did you knock the loft ladder over?" said Mrs. Brown.

William considered this, too.

"Well, I may've done," he said. "I sometimes think I walk in my sleep, an' when people walk in their sleep they don't know what they've done when they come out of it. I once heard of a man——"

"Be quiet."

"William!" said Mrs. Brown, in a voice of horror. "What a mess your bed's in!"

She drew down the chaotic bed-clothes to reveal William, lying in his pyjamas, clasping the bundled-up sheet under one arm.

"What on *earth* are you doing with that sheet?" she said.

William looked down at the sheet as if seeing if for the first time.

"Do you mean this?" he said.

"Of course your mother means that," snapped Mr. Brown. "What are you doing with it? Have you gone mad?"

It occurred to William that a pretence of insanity would provide a good way out of his difficulties, then reluctantly he abandoned the idea as involving too many complications.

"I prob'ly did it when I was walkin' in my sleep," he said. "I mus' have done. P'raps I was dreamin' I was in a buildin' that was on fire, an' I'd taken off my sheet to make a fire escape. I've heard of people makin' fire-escapes out of sheets in fires. They push their beds close to the window an' they tie one end of the sheet to the bed an'——"

"Be *quiet*," roared Mr. Brown, stemming the torrent as best he could. "Will you never learn a bit of sense? Waking the whole household at midnight, kicking ladders about the house! Here am I after a hard day's work"—he avoided the eyes that his family turned wonderingly upon him and substituted—"after a hard day's exertion, robbed of my sleep because you choose to play football with a loft ladder in the dead of night. If you won't think of me, you might think of your mother. Do you imagine it's pleasant for her, after standing in queues all day——"

"I haven't actually stood in a queue to-day, dear," said Mrs. Brown.

He waved this aside irritably.

"Do you imagine that your brother needs no sleep?"

Robert tried to look as if he hadn't been writing letters when the ladder fell.

"And your sister——"

"He might be in the coal hole," said Ethel, whose mind was still running on the burglar. "You never looked there."

"And Emily," went on Mr. Brown, noticing that Emily had joined the circle and not wishing to leave anyone out. "Are you aware that Emily has to be up by——" He realised that he didn't know what time Emily had to be up by and went on: "Has to be up long before you or any of us. Do you think she enjoys being awakened by your tomfoolery?"

"Don't worry about me, sir," said Emily gloomily. "It was you that waked me, talking on the landing, an', anyways, I've got far worse things than that to put up with in this 'ouse."

Mrs. Brown stifled a yawn. "Do let's get back to bed, dear," she said.

"Well, I hope you'll think over what I've been saying," said Mr. Brown, gazing sternly at his son, who sat up in bed, still clasping his sheet to his breast, an expression of wide-eyed wonder on his face. "And if I hear anything more from you to-night——"

"This morning," said Ethel.

"I shall deal with you very severely."

"Do go to bed, John," said Mrs. Brown. "I'll just straighten William's bed-clothes."

"You'll do nothing of the sort," said Mr. Brown. "If the boy chooses to make a shambles of his bed, he can deal with it himself. Come along back to bed, all of you, and let's try to get a little sleep."

They returned to their rooms, Mr. Brown's brow still dark with anger.

In the bedroom he turned to his wife.

"I'm going to *do* something about William," he said. "I won't have him in the house a day longer. I'll send him to sea, to the colonies, to an approved school——"

Mrs. Brown smiled at him.

"Now, John," she said, "you know how quickly time goes, and in a few years they'll all have left us and we'll be here alone and we'll look back on these days and think how happy we all were."

The grimness of his expression relaxed.

"Perhaps you're right, my dear," he said. "Come along. Let's get to bed."

Chapter 15

Ginger, Henry and Douglas were waiting for William at the gates of the Manor. Henry carried an empty bucket. They all carried sheets under their arms.

"Thought you were never coming," said Ginger.

"I had a bit of a job gettin' out," said William, and, summing up the situation as shortly as he could, added: "They stopped me gettin' out by the door, so I had to get out by that tree outside my window, an' it's a diff'cult sort of tree. Well, come on. Let's open the gates."

Henry tried them.

"They're locked," he said.

"They can't be," said Ginger.

"They weren't this morning," said Douglas.

"Let me try," said William.

He tried. They tried in turn. They tried all together. The gates remained locked.

"P'raps we'd better—sort of give it up," suggested Douglas.

"We're jolly well not going to," said William shortly. "Come on. We'll go round by the tadpole-pond hole."

They walked down the road to their familiar entrance and crawled through one after the other.

Then, in a silence broken only by stumbles,

ejaculations, and William's hoarse and penetrating admonitions to "shut up," they made their way to the house. There were no lights in any of the windows. It looked more gaunt and desolate and forbidding than ever.

"P'raps there's no one in," said Douglas. "It'd be a pity to waste a lot of time and trouble hauntin' it if there's no one in."

"Yes, there is," said Ginger. "Ole Monkey Face is in. Old Toad Face went out in the car an' he's not back yet, an' Monkey Face hasn't gone out at all. I've been watchin' from our house. You can see it nearly all from our house."

"Here's the coal chute thing," said William.

"We'll get jolly well messed up with coal goin' down it," said Douglas. "We'll be black."

"All the better for hauntin'," said William. "We could show black faces over our sheets. *Gosh!* It'd scare him stiff. . . . Come on." He had opened the flap of the coal hole. "I'll go first."

He vanished from sight. They waited for a few moments in silence, then:

"Are you all right, William?" said Ginger in a penetrating whisper.

"Yes. I've fallen on somethin' soft."

"P'raps it's coal dust."

"P'raps," said William uncertainly. "I can't see. You can come now. I'm gettin' out of the way."

One by one the other three slid down the chute.

"I'm goin' back to do it again," said Henry.

"No, you're not," said William, grabbing him. "We've come here to haunt, not play games."

"It *is* soft," said Ginger. "I don't think it's coal dust, either."

"Here's the light switch," said Douglas, who had been groping his way round the wall.

Light flooded the large bare cellar—bare, that is, but for the heaps of fur coats, furs and fur wraps that covered the floor.

The Outlaws looked at them without much interest.

"He's got a lot of furs," remarked William, summing up the situation.

"P'raps he feels the cold," said Ginger.

"I've got an aunt that feels the cold," said Douglas, "but she doesn't need all that much fur."

"P'raps he's goin' out to Russia or Iceland or somewhere," suggested Henry.

"Jolly good riddance!" said Ginger.

The suggestion satisfied them—they were not particularly interested in the problem, anyway—and they made their way to the door.

"There's a tap in this passage," said Henry. "Here it is! I'll fill my bucket."

He switched on the passage light, revealing a couple of packing-cases, piled high with furs.

"P'raps he's got them for Christmas presents for people," said Douglas. "He might have got a lot of aunts. . . ."

"Oh, come on," said William impatiently. "Now we go up these stairs and along this passage. Here's the main electric light switch, jus' by the door."

"We're goin' to turn that off, aren't we?" said Henry.

"Yes. I've done it. . . . Now come on. Through the door into the hall . . . I remember it quite well. . . ."

"You ought to," said Henry, "the number of times Miss Maurice let us play hide-an'-seek here!"

"Yes," said Douglas. "Do you remember the time when——? "

"Oh, shut up!" said William. "We've gotter be quiet now. . . . Here we are."

He opened the green baize door and they trooped silently into the hall. Moonlight poured through the high stained-glass windows, giving an eerie look to the carved chimney-piece, staircase and the suits of armour, whose visors seemed to be turned threateningly towards them. Several large wooden crates stood in one corner.

"Gosh!" whispered Douglas nervously. "P'raps it's haunted. . . ."

" 'Course it is," whispered William. "We're hauntin' it, aren't we? Now we've gotter go all over the house an' switch on all the light switches. That's the first thing to do."

They worked in silence till they had turned on all the downstairs switches.

"Seems funny the lights not comin' on," said Ginger.

" 'Course they don't, stupid," said William. "We've turned off the main switch, haven't we?"

"I know," said Ginger, "but it still seems sort of funny."

"We've finished downstairs. Now let's go upstairs."

They went up the broad moonlit staircase.

"I'll do this corridor," whispered William, "an' you do the other."

Faint clicks resounded through the silent house as one by one the switches were turned on. William listened for a moment outside each bedroom before he entered.

All were empty, till he reached the door at the end of the corridor, and from the door at the end of the corridor came the sound of deep rhythmic snores. Very very cautiously, very very silently, his tongue protruding from his lips, his brow wrinkled in the intensity of his efforts to control the natural exuberance of his movements, he opened the door and peeped inside. . . . The room was flooded with moonlight . . . and there in a large four-poster bed lay the man whom the Outlaws called Monkey Face and whom the Boss called Tonks, his eyes closed, his mouth open, sunk in sleep. On the table by his bed was an empty whisky bottle and a glass. The rigidity of William's face relaxed into a grin. He stretched out his hand, turned on the light switches by the door, then softly, silently, withdrew. . . .

Ginger, Henry, and Douglas were waiting for him on the half-landing.

"Have you done all yours?" whispered William.

They nodded.

"Well, come on, then," said William. "You remember what we fixed up to do next, don't you? You've gotter go down to the main switch, Douglas. It's jus' by that green baize door, you remember, an' you can fix the door open with a chair, so's you can see me, an' when I put up my arm once, you start turnin' it on an' off as quick as you can. An' Ginger's gotter stand behind that suit of armour with his rattle. You've got it, haven't you, Ginger?"

Ginger nodded and brought it out of his pocket.

"It's a jolly good one, too," he said, obviously preparing to display its merits.

"Shut up!" hissed William. "Don't start till you get the signal. I'll be jus' outside his room an' I'll put up both arms when I want you to start. You can do your moan all right, can't you?"

"Yes, I jolly well can," said Ginger, opening his mouth to prove it.

"Shut up," said William again. "Not yet . . . An' now we've got to get Henry up on the roof."

"It's goin' to be a bit difficult," said Henry.

"No, it's not," said William. "It's goin' to be jolly easy."

"I'd rather be outside than in," said Douglas. "It's sort of creepy in."

"I bet it's more creepy out," said Henry.

"Come on," said William impatiently. "There's a table an' a chair jus' under that skylight in the corridor. If we put the chair on the table, we'll soon get him out."

This proved a little more difficult and prolonged than William's optimism had allowed for. Once the whole erection crashed to the floor, and they waited in tense apprehension for a vengeful awakened Monkey Face . . . but no one appeared. The rhythmic snores continued unabated.

The erection was built up again, and Henry was, after many efforts, propelled through the skylight on to the roof. There was one perilous moment when he hung by his hands, dangling his legs, but the combined efforts of the other three pushed and prodded his solid person till it vanished from sight.

"Are you all right?" whispered William.

Henry's face, wearing a somewhat aggrieved expression, appeared in the aperture.

"I'm jus' about torn to pieces," he said bitterly.

"That doesn't matter," said William. "We'll hand up your bucket now."

He stood on the table, took the bucket from Ginger and handed it up to Henry.

"D'you know which his chimney is?" he asked.

"I think I do," said Henry, uncertainly.

THE SUITS OF ARMOUR ON THE STAIRCASE CAME
TO LIFE.

"Well, I'll knock on it, an', when you've found it, you knock back."

"All right," said Henry and vanished from sight.

"Now, get ready, all of you, an' we'll start," said William.

"Startin's all right," said Douglas, "but how's it goin' to end? In death, I shouldn't be surprised."

"Oh, shut up," said William.

Douglas went down to the green baize door, Ginger took up his position behind the suit of armour, William crept again along the corridor to Mr. Tonks's door.

Rhythmic snores still proceeded from it. Cautiously, William opened the door . . . Mr. Tonks still lay motionless, buried in sleep. Tiptoeing, holding his breath, William made his way over to the fireplace and tapped gently on the chimney. After a few moments an answering tap told him that Henry had located the chimney. He gave a sigh of relief, then crept back to the door, and, leaving the door wide open, took up his position and gave the first signal.

The sound of a rattle cut sharply through the air, and immediately afterwards a long, nerve-shattering, blood-curdling moan.

Tonks (alias too many names to enumerate), sat up in bed and looked about him. He'd been awakened by some sound, but he wasn't sure what sound. Then he knew . . . for almost immediately another blood-curdling moan rang through the silent house.

"Cripes!" said Tonks through chattering teeth. "I *knew* there was spooks about. I *told* him."

His first instinct was to plunge beneath the bed-clothes and remain hidden from whatever ghostly

menace stalked the house. Then the memory of the
Boss's face came to him, and he knew that he must
get out of bed and deal with whatever had to be dealt
with. Trembling, he got out of bed and approached the
door. Then his eyes gleamed wildly and the chattering
of his teeth sounded like so many castanets. The door
was open. He knew he'd shut it when he went to bed
and now it was open. . . .

"Blimey!" he moaned, then gave a high-pitched
scream of terror as a rush of soot and water came
pouring down the chimney into the fireplace.

His reluctance to leave the bedroom vanished
abruptly.

He made for the door, putting out his hand to the
switch. And then—while his hand was still a good foot
away from the switch—all the lights in the room burst
into a blaze of illumination.

"C-c-c-ripes!" squealed Tonks, reeling round and
staring about him in mounting terror. "*C-c-c-ripes!*"

The rest of the night was an experience that Tonks
never got straight in his mind for the rest of his life.
He tore madly about the house, lights going on and
off all about him, moans re-echoing, rattles rattling.
At one point a heap of slates fell from a skylight just as
he reached it. At another, ghostly white figures flitted
round him in the darkness. At another the suits of
armour on the staircase came to life and walked (rather
unsteadily) down the stairs. . . . It really lasted only
a few minutes, but it seemed to last for months, for
years. . . . He tore madly back to the bedroom, flung
on his clothes, and, running desperately through the
inferno of moans, rattles, sheeted figures and dancing
lights, gained the front door and vanished into the
night. . . .

Chapter 16

"Well, he's gone," said William. "We've done it!"

"What do we do next?" said Ginger. "Do we go an' tell Robert an' Gloria Gaye that it's ready for them?"

"I—I s'pose so," said William a little uncertainly.

His imagination had never carried him beyond the thrill of the haunting and the glorious moment of the tenant's eviction.

"Gosh! Didn't he look funny!" said Ginger.

For a moment or two they abandoned themselves to mirth—except Douglas.

"I think we ought to be gettin' home," he said. "I sort of feel that somethin' might *happen* if we don't."

"Of course," said William thoughtfully, "we've got a bit more straightening out to do. She never axshully *said* she'd marry him."

Ginger had wandered behind a screen in a corner of the hall.

"Gosh!" he said. "More furs! He must be jolly rich!"

"P'raps he's got an extravagant wife," suggested Henry, who had now come down from the roof and rejoined his friends.

"Tell you what!" said William. "Let's send some of

them to Gloria Gaye from Robert. I bet that'd make her want to marry him. They like furs."

"They like mink best," said Henry, with an air of worldly wisdom.

"How do you tell which is mink?" asked Ginger.

"They smell," said Douglas. "They smell awful."

"No, that's skunk, you idiot!" said William. "I know all about skunks. They——"

He stopped suddenly and stood listening, his face set and tense. "It's a car . . ." he said. "Put the light out, quick!"

Douglas leapt to the switch, and the hall was plunged in darkness, except where a shaft of moonlight fell on to the floor.

William looked cautiously out of the window. "It's ole Toad Face back," he said. "Come on! Quick! Upstairs!"

The four streaked upstairs and vanished round the bend of the staircase.

No sooner had they done this than the front door opened, and the man known as the Boss entered the hall. He went to the light and switched it on.

"Tonks!" he called.

There was no answer.

He raised his voice.

"*Tonks!*"

Scowling, he crossed the hall and went upstairs, taking the steps three at a time.

"*Tonks!*" he called again when he had reached the landing.

Still there was no answer. He strode to the bedroom at the end of the corridor. There he switched on the light and stood in the doorway, surveying the empty room, the tumbled unoccupied bed, the empty whisky bottle. He turned on his heel and went to the end of the corridor.

"Tonks! You drunken fool!" he bellowed.

His words re-echoed eerily through the passage, but there was no reply.

He stood there for a moment or two in silence . . . then through the silence came the sound of heavy vehicles on the drive. . . . He ran downstairs and threw open the hall door. Two lorries were just drawing up at the entrance.

A young man, with a smooth white face and protruding teeth, jumped down from the first.

"Jehosophat, Gaffer!" he said. "I'm glad to see you."

"Come on in, Syd," said the Boss shortly. "You're late."

"Late? We nearly didn't come at all. Lights flashing on and off. We saw 'em for miles."

"So did I," said the Boss grimly. "It put the wind up me, too."

"We thought it might have been some sort of signal to stay away."

"No, it was Tonks."

"Where is he?"

"Stretched out somewhere in the grounds by now, I suppose."

"Dead?"

"Dead drunk." He waved his hand towards the hall. "Get the stuff out of here. Quick."

"O.K., Gaffer," said Syd. He went to the door and called, "Come on, you geezers. Get this lot shifted."

A couple of men came in and began moving the packing-cases. Syd took down the screen and flung the furs into the middle of the floor. The Outlaws had crept to the half-landing and were peering down into the hall. Syd's voice, thin and nasal, reached them.

"Harry said to tell you that, with the Channel like it is, the consignment should reach the Belgian coast around dawn."

"Good!" said the Boss.

"How many furs have we got?" said Syd.

"Four hundred. They're expecting five hundred, but we had to call off Thursday's job."

"Ought to fetch a tidy bit of brass."

The two men were carrying the cases out to the lorry. Syd was counting and checking the loose furs, piling them at the foot of the stairs.

"There's more in the cellar," said the Boss. "Come on. Let's get them out."

They went through the green baize door, leaving the hall empty. . . . Slowly, cautiously, the Outlaws descended the stairs and stood in a little huddled group at the staircase foot.

"They're fur thieves," whispered William. "That's what they are."

"What can we do?" said Henry.

"We've gotter let the police know, somehow," said William. "We've gotter stop them takin' those furs to Belgium."

"Where's Belgium?" said Ginger.

"How should I know?" said William. "I'm not a fur thief."

The green baize door flew open, and each of the Outlaws made for the nearest shelter—Henry and Douglas behind chairs, William behind a packing-case, and Ginger behind the high carved settee.

Two men were coming through the door, carrying a crate. They set it down near William's packing-case and covered it with a pile of loose furs.

"Check my list, Boss?" said Syd.

"O.K. Come on!" said the Boss. "I wish you'd all get a move on. There's something about this place gives me the jitters."

William peered cautiously round from under the packing-case. Yes . . . the telephone was there on the table near where the Boss and Syd were standing. He almost chuckled to himself as one of his ideas came to him. It was quite easy to catch the eyes of Ginger, Henry and Douglas (the fur thieves were deeply absorbed in their lists) and by dint of gestures to make them understand that he was going to telephone the police and that they must make their way to the green baize door and escape. . . . Then followed a scene that an unconcerned spectator might have found somewhat bewildering. For, whenever the men went to the door with crates and armfuls of furs, four of the fur coats lying on the floor seemed suddenly to come to life and crawl swiftly across the hall—one towards the telephone table and three towards the baize doors—sprawling into immobility as soon as the men turned back into the room.

One of the men looked at them, scratching his head.

"Strike me pink!" he said. "The pesky things seem to move about."

"Stop talking and get on with the job," said the Boss shortly.

Progress was slow, but, inch by inch, the four progressed . . . till Ginger, Henry and Douglas were half-way across the hall and William was within reach of the telephone.

He waited till the Boss, Syd and the men were all out with the lorries, then reached up a hand, snatched the telephone from the table, and, holding it under his

WILLIAM REACHED UP A HAND AND SNATCHED THE
TELEPHONE.

coat, dialled 999. . . . . A voice answered him, but the men were already coming back, and he only had time to slip back the telephone on to the table before they entered the hall again.

The situation was becoming more and more dangerous, and the moment came when Syd returned from the lorry to find three fur coats lying on a rug that he had seen cleared of furs only a few moments before.

"Thought I told you to move that lot," he said to one of the men.

The man looked down at them in a puzzled fashion.

"Blimey! I *did* move 'em," he said.

"You darn well didn't," said Syd, grabbing at the nearest one. . . . Then he sprang back open-mouthed, with eyes starting from his head, as Ginger, Henry and Douglas emerged from their coats and made a dash for the green baize door. Recovering swiftly, he dived after them, but the three were through the door, and Ginger had slammed it to and shot the bolt home.

In an instant all was pandemonium. Syd put his shoulder to the green baize door and pushed. The Boss joined him. The other men ran out into the night.

William had slipped from his fur coat and was now concealed behind the crate. Fate, he felt, was closing in on him, but he thought that with luck he might escape through the front door under cover of the crate. He began to push it inch by inch across the hall. . . .

Then a heavy hand descended on him and someone grabbed him by the collar and yanked him to his feet. It was the Boss . . . William began to struggle, but a blow on the side of his head brought a whole constellation of stars before his eyes, and when they cleared he saw the two men coming in through the open front door, dragging Ginger, Henry and Douglas with them.

"Gosh!" said William,

"I told you," said Douglas, with gloomy triumph. "I *said* it was dangerous."

"Don't you worry," said William, stoutly. "We'll get out of it all right."

"Shut up, you!" said the Boss, providing a whole new constellation of stars with one swift movement of his hand.

*   *   *

They were in a lorry, bound tightly with ropes and gagged rather ineffectually with scarves and pullovers. William had already worked his gag loose and was gazing through a crack in the side of the lorry at the countryside through which they were passing.

" 'Spect we're nearly at the sea by now," whispered William to Ginger.

Then he looked down at his shoe. It was white. The phenomenon interested him. . . . He had watched the men pack the furs in sacks of flour and load the lorry with them. One of the bags must be leaking. Closer investigation proved that it was. He gave the sack an experimental kick with his foot.

"Go on," he whispered. "All of you, kick."

All of them kicked. The sides of the sack split open and the flour poured out, falling through a crack in the floor and leaving, presumably, a clear white trail along the country road.

The Outlaws worked hard and in silence. . . . They emptied the first sack and started on a second. Then:

"*Look!*" said William, peering out through the

back of the lorry. "Police cars. Gosh! I b'lieve they've picked us up. . . ."

What followed was amply embroidered by the Outlaws for weeks and months to come, but, in itself, it was so exciting as to need little embroidery. It was the sort of police car chase that William had seen, times innumerable, on the pictures and read of in thrillers, but in which he had never hoped to take part. They shot wildly from side to side, they zigzagged across the road, they swerved into lanes and out of lanes, and the police cars followed.

Then came the grand culmination of the whole evening. . . . The two police cars placed across the road . . . the wild swerve into a ditch . . . the glorious sight of the Boss, Syd and the two men being led ignominiously from the wreck of their lorry by three stalwart policemen, and the fourth policeman standing, looking down at the Outlaws, scratching his head, and saying:

"Strewth, am I dreaming or is there really four kids here?"

Chapter 17

The Outlaws, partially cleaned up, sat in a row on a bench in the police station, while a police sergeant summed up the story from his end of the adventure.

"We traced your call," he said, "and we found the marks of the lorries on the drive at the Manor, and we scoured the road till we caught up with the flour trail. Then we got all the mobiles out on the job and finished it off." He grinned at them. "I expect you were pretty relieved when you saw us."

"I was," said Douglas. "I was gettin' certain it would end in death."

"How did you come to be mixed up in it?" said the sergeant.

"Well, we were hauntin' a house," explained Ginger.

"Why?"

"Because we wanted bicycles."

"Seems a funny reason," said the sergeant.

"Well, you see, we wanted to get Robert married," said Henry, trying to make the situation clearer.

"I see," said the sergeant. "I mean, I don't. Whose idea was it?"

"William's," said Ginger.

"Which is William?"

"Him," said Ginger, pointing.

"What was the idea, William?"

William came out of a dream in which he was

reconstructing the whole story and moulding it nearer to the heart's desire. He had increased the four men to ten, and at present he was standing on a packing-case, flinging them off one by one as they attacked him. Half a dozen huddled inert figures lay about the floor of the hall. . . .

"What?" he said vaguely.

"Give us your account," said the sergeant.

"Well," said William, drawing a deep breath, "right from the beginnin' I thought there was somethin' suspicious about them. I knew they were crim'nals jus' with lookin' at 'em. They'd got crim'nal faces, so I did a bit of 'vestigatin'."

"Where?"

"In the grounds. Well, axshully, at the tadpole pond. An' he came along an'—well, he nearly left us for dead. We only jus' got away alive. You see, he knew we were on his track an' he wanted to do away with us, same as they do in books with people that are on their tracks. . . . So we thought we'd go along at night an' see what it was they were doin'. They might have been forgers or fur stealers or jus' murderers, but I had a sort of feeling all along that they were fur stealers. I've always thought I'd make a jolly good detective." He looked a little wistfully at the sergeant. "Do you think Scotland Yard will make me a detective now? I could work with the p'lice quite easily. I could come along after school every day, an' all day on Sat'days. I've got some jolly good ideas for catchin' crim'nals. I've got some new ones that haven't been tried out yet."

"We'll have to consider that," said the sergeant, looking at him with a twinkle.

"You see——" began William earnestly, but suddenly

a well-known voice cut through the conversation.

"I know me way, officer. Don't trouble to see me to me room. 'Ope you've 'ad the place done up since I was 'ere last. Time you laid 'ot and cold water on in me room, too. I'm not fussy but I like me comfort . . . Call me at nine o'clock with a nice cup o' tea an' a piece of bread an' butter. *Butter*, mind! None of yer marge."

They gazed wonderingly at the door as Mr. Rose entered, genial as ever, his ragged straw hat at a rakish angle over one eye. A policeman accompanied him. Mr. Rose did not seem at all surprised to see the Outlaws sitting in a row on a bench at the police station. Nothing ever surprised Mr. Rose.

He winked at William.

"Told you I'd show you what places you could sleep in fer nothin'," he said. "Well, this 'ere's one of 'em."

He passed on to a door in the further wall of the room, followed by the still wondering eyes of the Outlaws. At the door he turned and grinned at them.

"Thanks fer findin' me that nice 'ome this afternoon," he said. "I 'ad a good rest."

Then he vanished with his escort.

"Why is he here?" asked William.

"He was found climbing down the pear tree at the Hall," said the sergeant, "with half Mrs. Bott's jewellery in his pocket."

"Oh," said William thoughtfully.

"Well, we'd better think about getting you home," said the policeman. "Where do you live?"

It turned out that Ginger's, Henry's and Douglas's homes lay in one direction, and William's in another.

Two police cars drew up at the station. Ginger, Henry and Douglas piled themselves into one, while William took the seat next the driver in the other.

The car sped down the country road . . . past Honeysuckle Cottage, where Gloria Gaye slept fitfully, her trunks packed, the taxi that was to take her to the station ordered for eleven o'clock next morning . . . past the house where Rosalyn lay dreaming of a composite male figure compounded of Robert, Clark Gable, Gary Cooper and John Mills in about equal proportions, and where the black-and-white hat lay on the table by her bed, reduced to its component parts, for Rosalyn, becoming suddenly suspicious of Valerie's praise of it, had spent most of the evening taking it to pieces and putting it together again in different ways. . . past the Hall, where Mrs. Bott slept uncomfortably with all the cases that contained her jewels (she was taking no more chances) under her pillow . . . past the house where Valerie had fallen asleep in the act of searching in vain for "pineapple" in a book called *The Mystic Languages of Flowers* (she'd thought that perhaps it *meant* something and presumably even pineapples bore flowers at some stage of their existence) . . . past the Vicarage, where the Vicar, ever hopeful, had, just before he went to bed, entered Gloria Gaye's name among his subscribers to the Church Restoration Fund with a question mark after it. Oddly enough, he was dreaming of the question mark, and it was, in his dream, growing larger and larger and larger. . . .

"I expect they'll give you something for to-night's work," the policeman was saying to William. "What do you want most?"

"A bicycle," said William without hesitation.

"I expect you'll get it. Anything else?"

William looked at him, and, to his surprise, found that he wasn't joking.

"Well, there's one other thing . . ." he said slowly.

"What is it?" said the policeman.

William told him.

The policeman threw back his head with a roar of laughter.

"All right," he said. "I'm game."

"Thanks awfully," said William. "It's jolly decent of you."

They were approaching the Lanes' house now. The police car drew to a stop at the gate. William got out and went up the moonlit path to the house. Then he took a handful of small pebbles from the garden bed by the door and threw them at a certain window. After some minutes the window was drawn up, and the pallid, sleepy face of Hubert Lane appeared.

"Who is it?" he said. "What's the matter?" He looked down at William. "What d'you want, William Brown?"

"Well, I told you I worked with the p'lice an' you wouldn't b'lieve me."

"No, an' I don't still," said Hubert. "What are you doing here, anyway? It's the middle of the night."

"I'm jus' comin' back from one of my jobs," said William. "Thought I'd jus' give you a call an' see how you were. Well, I can't stay any longer. Good night."

He turned and went back to the car . . . and Hubert gaped and goggled as he saw the policeman, standing to attention, open the door of the car for William and salute him smartly as he got into his seat. It drove off again down the country road, and William, a grin of delight on his face, turned to look back at Hubert's pyjama-ed figure still hanging out of the window. The moonlight showed his staring eyes and his mouth wide open in amazement. . . .

They were approaching the Browns' house now, and something of William's exuberance faded.

"I say," he said nervously, "you'd better not come up to the door. I'll get in an awful row if they know I've been out."

"Do you think that in the circumstances you will?" asked the policeman.

"Gosh, yes!" said William earnestly. "You don't know my father. He was mad with me jus' before I came out, 'cause of a ladder that fell down by itself jus' when I happened to be walkin' along a passage. He's a very unreas'nable man."

"You'd really rather I didn't come in and explain?" said the policeman.

"*Gosh*, yes!" said William, horrified by the idea.

"They'll have to know some time."

"Yes, that's all right," said William, "but he gets mad when he's waked up sudd'nly in the night. He's a bit—jus' a *bit* more reas'nable in the morning, but in the middle of the night he's awful. You should have heard him carryin' on at me, jus' 'cause this ladder fell down by itself when I happened to be walkin' along the passage."

"How will you get in?" said the policeman.

"I've got a way," said William. "I got out by it all right."

"Very well," said the policeman, trying to hide his amusement. "Just as you like."

He drew up in the shadow of the trees and watched William as, coat collar turned up, shoulders hunched,

his hand held out as if it clasped a revolver, he crept
furtively from bush to bush on his way to the house.

*   *   *

The Browns were assembled in the drawing-room,
wearing dressing-gowns and discussing Williams disappearance with an exasperation that was perhaps natural
in the circumstances and a secret anxiety that they tried
in vain to stifle.

Waking in the early hours of the morning and
remembering the chaotic state in which she had left
her younger son's bed, Mrs. Brown had slipped out
of her bedroom without waking her husband and gone
along to William's bedroom to make sure that some
sort of order had been evolved from the chaos and
that he was not "catching his death."

She found the bed empty and the sheet missing.

Mr. Brown, roused from sleep and informed
of what had happened, burst forth in a fury that
roused every other member of the household except
Emily. Realising that no more sleep was possible, they
assembled in the drawing-room to discuss the situation,
or rather to listen to Mr. Brown's pungent comments
on it.

"Of course the boy was up to some mischief from
the start," he said. "He was making his way out with
that sheet when he knocked the ladder over."

"I shall be a wreck to-morrow," said Ethel
dispassionately.

"We'll all be wrecks," said Mr. Brown.

"But, darling, something *might* have happened
to him," said Mrs. Brown.

"Something *will* happen to him," said Mr. Brown
grimly.

"He might—he might have been kidnapped," said Mrs. Brown. "One reads things in the newspapers."

"Kidnapped!" said Mr. Brown with a harsh laugh. "Kidnapped! That's good!"

"Who'd want him?" said Robert succinctly.

"Perhaps we ought to ring up the police," said Mrs. Brown.

"Police!" echoed Mr. Brown with another harsh laugh. "We shall probably see all we want of the police before we're through. Heaven only knows what the boy's up to."

"It certainly is very naughty of him," sighed Mrs. Brown. "He must have got out through the bedroom window. It was wide open. I shut it because the night air was making his room quite chilly."

"It's outrageous," said Mr. Brown. "Absolutely outrageous. That a child of that age should—should make a *shambles* of an entire household! It's—well, it's *outrageous*. I shall take very firm steps over this. I'll teach the boy a lesson he won't forget."

Mrs. Brown sighed again.

"It's so late," she said, "and he's only a little boy. I *do* hope nothing's happened to him."

"What could have happened?" said Mr. Brown impatiently. "The boy's obviously off on some piece of mischief. He's taken his sheet with him, which proves that he'd arranged some prank or other. What *could* have happened to him?"

There was a silence, during which all four, in order to counter the secret anxiety that lay heavy at their hearts, tried to whip up their anger against William.

"Outrageous!" growled Mr. Brown once more, pacing to and fro.

"He's *quite* impossible," said Ethel. "I'm sure he was behind that business of Henry and Douglas this afternoon."

"It might have been a kind thought," said Mrs. Brown. "I mean, flowers and a chocolate box . . . I often think he means well."

"He's been messing about in my affairs, too, to-day," said Robert darkly, remembering Rosalyn's cryptic reference to the "innocent child".

"Pull back the curtain, Robert," said Mrs. Brown, "so that we can see the garden."

Robert pulled back the curtain, then stood at the window, staring upward.

"Good *Lord!*" he said.

"Yes?"

"I could swear I saw him shinning up that tree. I bet you anything he's trying to get back into his bedroom that way."

The crash of breaking glass confirmed his words, as William, unaware that his mother had closed the window, tried to swing himself through it from the nearest branch. Then, recovering himself, he dropped from branch to branch till he landed in safety on the moonlit lawn.

It was Robert who ran out, grabbed him and dragged him through the french window. For a few seconds the four dressing-gowned figures stood and looked at him in silence. Then Mrs. Brown said:

"Are you hurt, William?"

"No," said William a little regretfully, dismissing a mental vision of the family weeping round his death-bed, expressing deep contrition for all their past unkindness.

And then the storm broke. As all the Browns

talked at once and kept interrupting each other, William couldn't hear what each was saying, though the general drift of their remarks was clear enough.

"Disgraceful!"

"Outrageous!"

"—your mother's anxiety . . ."

"—a severe lesson . . ."

". . . hardly a wink of sleep . . ."

"What were you thinking of to——"

"—disturbing the whole household . . . unpardonable behaviour . . ."

"—once and for all . . ."

"—those flowers—chocolate box——"

"When I was a boy I'd never have dreamed of——"

"—constant nuisance of yourself——"

"And the *sheet*, William," wailed Mrs. Brown.

Whenever there was a lull in the storm, William began, "But listen——" Then the storm would break out again, drowning whatever he had to say.

Once he got as far as "I've been catchin' crim'nals . . ." but another "Outrageous!" from Mr. Brown strangled the words at birth.

Then Mr. Brown secured silence by a sweeping gesture of authority and said:

"Now, go straight to bed, William. I'll deal with you in the morning."

William, who had given up the unequal struggle to gain a hearing, and realised that he'd had a tiring day and that bed would be welcome, muttered, "Oh, all right," and, going into the hall, began to mount the stairs.

The Browns stood at the bottom of the staircase, watching him sternly.

At the third step he turned.

"I say, I'm jolly hungry," he said. "Can I have a piece of cake?"

"No," said Mr. Brown.

"Oh, all right," muttered William.

He went up three more steps, then turned round again.

"I'm jolly thirsty," he said, realising this, too. "Can I have a drink of lemonade?"

"No!" said Mr. Brown.

"Oh, all right," muttered William.

He went up three more steps then turned again as a sudden memory struck him.

"I say! I left my aeroplane in the garden. Can I fetch it 'case it rains?"

"*No!*" said Mr. Brown.

"Oh, all right," muttered William.

As he turned to go up the few remaining stairs, a series of yelps and barks came from the back of the house.

Jumble, who never slept well during a full moon, had become aware that something unusual was afoot and wanted to be in it. Moreover, he had discovered a bone that he had mislaid for some weeks and was eager to show it to William.

William turned round.

"I say! Can I have Jumble in to sleep with me?"

Mr. Brown advanced to the foot of the staircase.

"If—you—say—one—more—word——" he said, threateningly.

"Oh, all right," muttered William and vanished into his bedroom.

And then came four loud authoritative knocks on the front door.

The Browns stood and stared at it helplessly.

"The police!" said Robert.

"It only needed this," said Mr. Brown in a tone of stoical resignation.

"Perhaps if we give them a drink . . ." said Mrs. Brown, with vague memories of soothing irate wardens who came to complain of black-out irregularities during the war.

"Don't you dare give them any of my whisky," said Mr. Brown.

"But if it is to get William out of trouble——"

"Nothing can do that."

"If you must give him a drink," said Robert, "there's that bottle of British sherry."

Ethel threw a glance at herself in the hat-stand mirror, and, assuming her most winsome expression, went to open the door.

A policeman stood on the threshold.

*   *   *

The policeman had waited in his car in order to watch developments. He had not heard the breaking of William's window or seen his ignominious reunion with his family, but he had heard the raised voices of the Browns and had gathered that all was not going well with the returned wanderer.

He looked at the four dressing-gowned figures and finally fixed his gaze on Mr. Brown.

"You're Mr. Brown?" he said.

"I am," admitted Mr. Brown.

"I've come about your son, William."

"I knew it," groaned Mr. Brown. "Come in."

The policeman came in.

"Will you have a drink?" said Mrs. Brown. "There's whisky"—then, meeting the eye that her husband rolled in her direction, added hastily—"or perhaps you prefer British sherry?"

"Nothing for me, thank you, madam. I just came to tell you——"

"Whatever he's done, he didn't *mean* to," said Mrs. Brown.

"Let's get it over," said Mr. Brown. "What *has* he done?"

The policeman told them what he'd done . . . then, having answered the resultant fire of questions as well as he could, took his departure. . . .

The Browns stood and stared at each other.

"I always *said* he meant well," said Mrs. Brown triumphantly.

"That boy's a credit to the family," said Mr. Brown. "I knew he'd got it in him, of course. The rest of you never gave the child a chance."

"The—the *courage* of it!" said Robert. "He always was a plucky kid."

"It was so sweet of him to send me those flowers," said Ethel, whose memories of the day were naturally by this time a little confused, "and, after all, why *shouldn't* he use his garters for catapults?"

"Come on, Mary," said Mr. Brown, starting towards the staircase. "Let's go up to him."

"One minute, dear," said Mrs. Brown, hurrying into the kitchen and taking from a tin a large cake that she had made that evening for the Women's Institute cake-making competition.

"Come on, Ethel," said Mr. Brown, but Ethel was also in the kitchen mixing a glass of lemonade.

"Where's Robert?" said Mr. Brown, feeling that the family should go to congratulate William in a body.

Robert had run into the garden to fetch William's aeroplane.

Mr. Brown hesitated, then went to open the back door and let in Jumble. Jumble leapt in exultantly, carrying the bone in his mouth.

"Aren't you coming, John dear?" said Mrs. Brown, who was now at the foot of the staircase with the cake.

"One minute, dear," said Mr. Brown and went to the sideboard cupboard to take out a box of dates that William had been forbidden to touch.

"Wait for me," said Ethel, running to the drawer in the bureau where she kept her sweet ration.

William sat up in bed and blinked as the strange procession entered his bedroom—Mrs. Brown with the cake, Ethel with the lemonade and chocolate, Robert with the aeroplane, Mr. Brown with the dates and, bringing up the rear, Jumble with his bone.

"*Gosh!*" he said weakly, thinking that he must be dreaming.

But the next few minutes convinced him that he wasn't.

"And now, darling," said Mrs. Brown at last, "tell us all about it."

And then, as well as he could through mouthfuls of cake, chocolate and dates, gesticulating so dramatically in illustration of his story that he knocked over the lemonade and hit Jumble on the nose, William told them all about it. . . .

*　　*　　*

The sound of the returning police car roused Mr. Heppleback from his slumbers. He got out of bed and went to the window. He had spent the afternoon with

"AND NOW, DARLING," SAID MRS. BROWN, "TELL US
ALL ABOUT IT."

Emily, sitting by the river, while she described to him the various stages of an obscure disease from which one of her aunts had once suffered, and finally invited him to accompany her to a second cousin's funeral on Tuesday. Mr. Heppleback had enjoyed the afternoon. He had a healthy man's interest in obscure diseases and he always enjoyed funerals. . . . But his thoughts were not with Emily. He was gazing at the Browns' house, which could be seen quite plainly through the trees from his cottage. There was evidently much coming and going in the Browns' house. There were lights in the rooms, figures moving to and fro. . . . But that did not interest Mr. Heppleback.

What interested Mr. Heppleback was two jagged holes in the smooth moonlit surface of two of the windows.

He went to his coat, which hung behind the door, and took from its pocket the book in which he made his notes for the next week's work. Slowly and carefully he wrote:

Mr. Brown.
Hall window: 2 ft. 6 ins. × 1 ft. 6 ins.
Bedroom window: 4 ft. 4 ins. × 2 ft. 6 ins.

THE END